THE GREATEST JEWISH AMERICAN LOVER IN HUNGARIAN HISTORY

MICHAEL BLUMENTHAL

ALSO BY MICHAEL BLUMENTHAL

No Hurry: Poems 2000–2012

Sympathetic Magic: Poems

Days We Would Rather Know: Poems

Laps: A Book-Length Poem

Against Romance: Poems

To Woo and To Wed: Poets on Love & Marriage (editor)

Weinstock Among the Dying: A Novel

When History Enters the House: Central European Essays,
1992-1996

Dusty Angel: Poems

And Yet: Selected Poems of Péter Kántor

All My Mothers and Fathers: A Memoir

Correcting the World: Selected Poetry and Writings
of Michael Blumenthal

And: Poems

Unknown Places: Poems by Péter Kántor (translator)

Just Three Minutes, Please: Thinking Out Loud on National
Public Radio

"Because They Needed Me": The Incredible Struggle of
Rita Miljo to Save the Baboons of South Africa

THE GREATEST
JEWISH AMERICAN LOVER
IN HUNGARIAN HISTORY

STORIES

MICHAEL BLUMENTHAL

etruscan press

Etruscan Press
Wilkes University
84 West South Street
Wilkes-Barre, PA 18766
(570) 408-454

WILKES
UNIVERSITY

www.etruscanpress.org

Published 2014 by Etruscan Press
Printed in the United States of America
Cover design by Michael Ress
Interior design and typesetting by Laurie Elizabeth Powers
The text of this book is set in Times New Roman.

First Edition

14 15 16 17 18 5 4 3 2 1

Library of Congress Cataloguing-in-Publication Data

Blumenthal, Michael
  [Short stories. Selections]
  The greatest Jewish American lover in Hungarian history / Michael Blumenthal.
    pages cm
  Summary: "Blumenthal draws both a humorous and heartrending portrait of expatriate life in Europe and Central Europe, as well as the hazards and confusions that
confront a European sensibility living in contemporary America. In venues as diverse
as Israel, Hungary, Paris, Cambridge and, even, Texas, the stories testify to the work
of an American in an increasingly connected and globalized world"-- Provided by
publisher.
  ISBN 978-0-9886922-4-4 (pbk.)
  1. Short stories, Jewish. I. Title.
  PS3552.L849G74 2014
  813'.54--dc23

Please turn to the back of this book for a list of the sustaining funders
of Etruscan Press.

for Isabelle & Noah,
this not-so-great Jewish-American lover's greatest loves

"I had affairs with a few girls of my own age, and they taught me that no girl, however intelligent and warm-hearted, can possibly know or feel half as much at twenty as she will at thirty-five."

— Stephen Vizinczey, *In Praise of Older Women: The Amorous Recollections of András Vajda*

Author's Note

In my "real" life, I am a law professor, pledged and committed to seeking and finding the truth as best as we mere lawyerly humans can, and helping those who are its possible beneficiaries. In my "other" life, I am a writer, committed to another kind of truth—perhaps deeper, more nuanced, and certainly often more difficult to achieve—and to the pleasure and moral self-scrutiny of my readers.

What follows are works of fiction, howsoever they may depend for their genesis and some of their details on actual occurrences and actual people in my life, myself included. What they are decidedly *not*, dear readers, are mere autobiographical vignettes disguised as something else. We fiction writers are *not*, like Bartleby, copyists—we are, rather, embellishers, inventors, liars, exaggerators, people who, as the poet, Robert Pack, once put it, tell personal lies in order to tell impersonal truths. The fiction writer and the lawyer, blessedly, bow to different gods, and I try, in my happily divided life, to remain devout to those I worship in each domain. So—here's hoping you will worship with me, and not find yourself expecting to encounter the wrong god in the wrong place, as I hope I haven't either.

The Greatest Jewish American Lover in Hungarian History

Acknowledgments

Several of the stories included in this selection have previously appeared in the following periodicals, to whose editors the author is profoundly grateful.

The Chattahoochee Review	"Tomorrow"
Formations	"The Translator"
International Literary Quarterly	"Three Beds"
Legal Studies Forum	"The Life You Hate May Be Your Own"
One Story	"The Death of Fekete"
Ploughshares	"She and I"
Story Quarterly	"He Had Tried"

I would also like to express my deep gratitude to Phil Brady, Jackie Fowler and all the other good people at Etruscan Press, who bravely fight on against the combined forces of conglomerate publishing, the bullying homogenization of taste, the relentless noise of self-promotion, and the many other deeply mixed blessings the twenty-first century has brought to those who love, and try to create, literature. And thanks, also, to my friend Jim Elkins for his expert proofreading and equally expert editorial advice.

THE GREATEST JEWISH AMERICAN LOVER
IN HUNGARIAN HISTORY

MICHAEL BLUMENTHAL

THREE BEDS

The boy, hardly nineteen, was the son of a famous Israeli sculptor David Yogev and his beautiful, much younger, wife Sarah. He was a beautiful young man as well, and, what's more, intelligent and athletic in the bargain, possessed of the kind of calm and reticence even very few adult men could pride themselves on. So it was no wonder that older women—particularly those afflicted with unhappy marriages or sexually disinterested husbands—took an interest in him.

It was no wonder, also, that Daphna Feuerstein, who had seduced his far shyer and less attractive older brother, Etan, several months earlier, would begin to show an interest in him as well. The two boys' bedrooms in their parents' Tel Aviv apartment on En Harod Street were only inches apart and the temptation for an attractive woman of thirty-five to parade around in various states of undress in front of two hardly post-adolescent young men was simply too great to resist.

He had had girlfriends before—too many for a boy his age, some family friends insisted—but his father had been a young man of notoriously varied romantic experience, so it was no surprise that the branch hadn't fallen far from the tree. His older brother,

Etan, had also inherited a great deal from his father. But in his case it was the sensitive and artistic (and, insofar as the details of the quotidian life were concerned, mostly dysfunctional) side. Already a published poet and accomplished watercolor painter by his twentieth birthday, the young man was possessed of a radically otherworldly air, complete with a state of physical dishevelment and untidiness that made him far less attractive to women than his popular and exceedingly well-adjusted brother—skier and windsurfer *par excellence*, star student, budding veterinarian, and already what the American rock and roll legend Elvis Presley might have called *a hunk a hunk of burning love.*

Daphna Feuerstein had been Etan's first lover, and it rendered matters no less untidy within the Yogev family that, in addition to being the mother of three young children, she was also David Yogev's best friend's daughter. She was also nearly fifteen years older than the young virgin she had so eagerly taken to bed, and nearly seventeen years older than his younger brother, to whom, she liked to think, she would have far less to teach.

Whatever it was she had, or didn't have, to teach young Simon Yogev, she figured, she would have plenty of time to find out. She planned on this being a long relationship—far longer, at least, than the one with his brother Etan had been. As she saw it, it had more potential. She loved the scent of Simon's body, the taste of his semen, she loved the soft furry hair on his legs and his lithe, muscular chest, and, perhaps above all, she loved the tight black curls on his head, loved running her fingers through them when they made love, and loved, even, the silence with which he responded to her forceful vocal demonstrations of ecstasy and pleasure.

Her estranged husband, Hanan, was an artistic and attractive man too—*and* had gradually become rich in the bargain. When they first met at a Tel Aviv nightclub, he had been a struggling jazz musician, a man who had an easy way with women and a difficult time paying the bills. Then, once their first son was born, he had decided that the combined life of a struggling artist and a family man wasn't for him, and, spotting a void in Tel Aviv's booming economy, had opened a bicycling messenger service catering to the new boom in internet and high-tech companies. Soon there was plenty of money to go with the music.

Their other two children, a boy and a girl named Rami and Timla, had been born in rapid succession, and soon thereupon there followed a large house in Tel Aviv's airy and affluent Jaffa district. They seemed to have it all: looks, money, three beautiful children. The kind of couple others—Simon and Etan's mother among them—pointed to with a combination of adulation and envy.

But, as was almost always the case, cracks and crevices were forming just beneath the smooth veneer of the enviable. Though hardly inexperienced during her adolescent years in Tel Aviv, Oslo and Budapest (her father was an Israeli-born Hungarian, her mother a Norwegian), Daphna Flinker had married young—at hardly twenty—and had her first child just before her twenty-second birthday. Two children and ten years later, with her husband spending more and more of his time and energy emptying bills from the pockets of bicycle messengers and less and less on her, she had begun to feel she was missing something—sex above all—and she knew that, just below the portrait of the loving, beautiful, and happily married young mother she presented to

5

the world, another canvas was beginning to take shape: that of a embittered young woman filled with unrequited hungers and unanswered cravings.

She was also a painter, and not without a modicum of talent, so that her small initial intimacies with Etan Yogev often focused on their shared artistic passion, as well as her comfortable, almost familial, friendship with his parents. She saw him as a young Chagall, herself as Frieda Kahlo (she even looked, a bit, the part—a kind of Latino *sabra*); she perceived him as a wild mop of hair that needed taming and felt herself a temptress eager and willing to domesticate it.

Etan Yogev had had no experience in bed—and hardly any outside of it—and it was not without a strong feeling of awkwardness and insecurity that he had first allowed Daphna Flinker to guide his somewhat ambivalent member into her own body, and his lips against her lips. She enjoyed it—this teacherly role—it had been a very long time since she had been able to practice the art of sexual instruction, and there was something exciting and alluring about this—all that innocence in a single place! Yes, he was unkempt, disorderly, possessed of an air of distraction, but nonetheless—nonetheless!—there was something—how else could she put it?—something *adorable* about him. She imagined that he closely resembled his father as a young man . . . and just look what had become of him!

As for young Etan, he had found it confusing at first—so much closeness to an actual human being! He had been reading about such pleasures for so long—so many Madame Bovarys and Anna Kareninas, so many lustful and tragic romantic heroines (even, from America, the occasional Edna Pontellier, parrots urging her on from their cages)—that the actual experiencing of one hardly seemed as novel, or exciting, as one might have imagined for a young boy losing his innocence to an older, more experienced, woman. What's more, his younger brother had always been the one the girls were interested in, allowing his own romantic life to remain abstract and imaginary. And that was just the way he might—had he reflected upon such matters at all— have preferred it.

The day he had kissed Daphna for the first time they had ridden their bikes to the Sea of Galilee for a swim. It was late August—just at the height of Israeli summer before the High Holy Days—and the air was crisp and clear, the water revivifying, even shockingly, cold. Even he couldn't help notice how lovely she was—even lovelier in a bathing suit where one could see, or imagine, all of her. She was small and dark, with fiery, passionate eyes and a little-girl-like laugh that suggested someone far younger than her years. And then there was her skin—dark, well-oiled, beckoning. It seemed to him like the skin of the heroines of the great romantic novels. It made him timid, but it also made something just below his waist begin to tingle.

When they lay together on the grassy shore of Galilee after emerging from the water, she placed a hand on his leg, stroking the thin hairs. Then she began kissing his neck, caressing his feet with her own. It felt good—no, it felt *very* good. And— awkwardly, timidly, ineptly at first—he responded, with her more than willing to show the way.

David and Sarah Yogev, like many members of the Israeli artistic and intellectual elite, were libertines insofar as their children's sexual experience was concerned. So it was not so much disturbing that their almost twenty-one-year-old son was sleeping with their best friend's married daughter in their house as it was bizarre—particularly for Sarah Yogev—to be suddenly awoken to the pleasure-induced moans of a woman whose three young children and their father she had fed at her table just weeks before. She wasn't sure what she felt—Was it betrayal? Jealousy? Merely confusion? But one thing she knew for certain: She didn't like it. Why couldn't her older son, like his younger brother before him, simply choose an *appropriate* young virgin with whom to first experience the pleasures of the flesh?

But, then, she reasoned, nothing *else* about her elder son had ever been appropriate—why should this be? She too had had her share of wild times, after all. As a twenty-five-year-old girl, she had gone to Paris for the express purpose of seducing the twenty-five year-older famous sculptor who was to become the boys' father. And there had been plenty of amorous adventures prior to that as well. So why deny her young sons theirs? And, after several months, urged on by the obvious bemusement and vicarious pleasure her husband felt at this turn of events, she had even begun to get used to the idea.

"Elle a quand même un beau cul," David Yogev would remark in French, suggesting that certain of the more admirable portions of Daphna's anatomy had not entirely escaped his attention. *"Non, pas du tout,"* his wife was forced to admit. Her husband, she recalled, had always been particularly fond of nice asses. Before gravity had begun to exact its inevitable toll, she had even been possessed of one of her own.

As a young couple in Paris—or, rather, as a young woman and a significantly older man—she and David often sat in cafés and played what they affectionately called "the three-bed game." Each one would name an artist or intellectual in Tel Aviv whom they knew (a man for him, a woman for her) and then—by going through a list of the lovers they each knew their selection to have had—they could usually determine that the two people they had chosen were *never* more than three beds apart! So incestuous was the world of the Israeli intelligentsia! So one had to admit that the story of Daphna Flinker and Etan Yogev seemed to fit right in.

The real trouble, however, only began when Daphna's attentions and ministrations began to shift from Etan to his younger brother. It had begun rather subtly—with her often sitting beside Simon, rather than Etan, at the dinner table, followed by what seemed longer and longer periods, during her visits with the children to the Yogev's Galilee week-end home; that the two of them were absent from the house altogether. Then there were the glances, the seemingly accidental touches, all the signs Sarah Yogev could so well recognize from her own younger years.

Daphna and Simon, of course, had done their best to make it seem as if there had been a full stop, followed by a long ellipse rather than a mere segue, that separated her relationships with the two brothers. The facts, however, belied such an explanation. Simon Yogev well remembered the first night Daphna Flinker had come to his bed in his parents' Tel Aviv apartment. There had been a quiet dinner downstairs—his mother's famous Hungarian goulash followed by her equally famous cheese-and-apricot strudel—during which he couldn't help notice that Daphna's gaze, rather than being directed at his older brother, was perpetually fixed on him, and that, from across the table, her feet brushed against his more frequently than mere chance might have allowed.

That night, sleeping rather fitfully, he woke to the rustling of his own sheets and the warm, not unfamiliar, feeling of a woman's flesh beside him, and then of equally warm lips descending his chest toward his still-sleeping member, accompanied by a feminine voice whispering sweetly in Hebrew, *Ahuvi Simon… ahuvi, ahuvi, ahuvi.* What had followed from that was the inevitable—a night filled with such fantastically lubricated lust and tenderness that not even a glimmer of fraternal loyalty could interfere with its pleasures. In the morning he would have to, as some writer his father liked—perhaps it was the Frenchman Zola?—had written, "swallow his large toad of nausea and regret," in any event. There was now little question as to what Daphna Flinker's real desires had been: Simon's brother had merely been a way station en route to her actual goal, and now she had attained it. But, even before this, a certain unspoken tension between the brothers had long been in the air—how could it *not* have been? It would be devastating to his older brother, Simon thought guiltily (he was well acquainted with the story of Cain and Abel), from whom he had already stolen most of the future family glory, to have his first lover taken from him by his brother as well?

She would simply *break up* with Etan, she promised him, she would tell him what perhaps had become obvious to him already—that, painting or no painting, they really didn't have very much in common, that she didn't really feel the relationship was good for either of them in the long run, and so on and so forth. (How then, Simon wondered, would she explain why the relationship was good for the two of *them*?)

But beneath Simon Yogev's veneer of otherworldliness there lay rather acute powers of intuition and observation. He had sensed Daphna's impending flight from his sheets in favor of his brothers' even before it had actually taken place. He may have looked like Heinrich Hoffmann's *Struwwelpeter*, but he was possessed of his father's foresight and intuition. And he could feel, nightly, the sense of Daphna's flesh, as well as her attentions, unwinding from his own.

Living in two almost entirely separate worlds—Etan in the world of intellect and art, Simon in that of sports and women—whatever rivalry might ever have existed between the brothers previously had been contained mostly below the surface. At times, Etan had even ventured a foray into his younger brother's territory—as, for example, several years earlier, when he had taken up swimming and bicycling with a vengeance, managing to join the annual summer swim all the way across the Galilee. In the process, he had also developed a body far more muscular and sculpted physique than his disheveled, unkempt coiffure and otherworldly gaze might have suggested.

But each seemed dominant within his own sphere, into which the other dared not tread, and Simon Yogev had always taken it for granted than his older brother—if he could somehow survive the daily tasks of paying the bills and doing his laundry—was heir apparent to their father's artistic gifts, even if not to his capacities with women and soccer balls.

So that Etan Yogev's little romance with Daphna Flinker, in addition to providing his mother with a few sleepless nights, had provided a not entirely unwelcome realignment of the status quo, and *that*, if nothing else, had provided Sarah Yogev with a certain welcome relief: Perhaps her older son, after all, was not doomed to a life of being cared for by his mother, or by some doughty, desperate young woman sufficiently enamored of his artistic gifts to overlook the absence of most others. Perhaps he would still grow up to be "normal," whatever that meant.

So, when the transition from the older brother's bed to the younger's openly took place, the fault lines between fantasy and reality suddenly split open as well, and, with them, the relative peace and contentment that had, for some months, characterized the Yogev family's winter and early spring came to an end. Now it was not only Simon's potentially wrecked future (Daphna Flinker, Sarah Yogev feared, was ripe for motherhood yet once again), but his older brother's apparently fractured ego that needed tending to, not to mention the Cold War-like mini-détente that now erected a kind of psychological Berlin Wall between the two brothers' sleeping quarters as well as in their day-to-day relations.

Etan, to put it simply, was heartbroken, his brother guilt-ridden, their briefly shared concubine triumphantly radiant.

Like someone moving backwards through the seven stages of grief, Sarah Yogev slowly moved from her initial state of shock and disbelief, followed reluctantly by acceptance and hope, to profound depression, followed by unmitigated anger at her younger son and his much older girlfriend, and then by a profound sense of guilt toward her fragile and hyper-sensitive older son for having allowed the liaison with a so much older—and still married!—woman to go on to begin with. Now the bargaining stage was about to begin, but it was not yet clear to her where on the table her chips lay, or whether, perhaps, simple denial might be the wiser course.

One thing she decidedly *didn't* want, she kept reminding herself as she was once again confronted—at an even higher volume—with Daphna Flinker nightly (and occasionally mid-afternoon) orgasmic elocutions from upstairs, was a grandchild at this point in her life, much less three step-grandchildren to go with it. So she rather unsubtly placed a package of condoms right beside Simon's bed and another in the bathroom cabinet where he kept his shaving things. There were no lengths, she reminded herself, a desperate woman wouldn't go to in order to hold onto a man she loved . . . particularly if that man happened to be only a boy.

As for David Yogev, his sincere concern over his older son's fragile and wounded ego was somewhat mitigated by the bemusement—and, indeed, admiration—with which he observed his friend's daughter navigate, and escape seemingly unscathed from, the various romantic minefields that lay in her path. He had always been intrigued by rebels and anti-moralists—Raskolnikov had always been his favorite literary character, along with Julien Sorel—having long been one himself. This girl was not merely, he thought (a small but undeniable glimmer of paternal envy running through him) a marvelous conquest . . . she had *hutzpah* to boot. She knew what she wanted, or at least desired, and was determined to get it. How convincingly could a man like himself argue with that?

Clearly, his younger son, guilt and all, was hardly unhappy with these new amorous developments either. Hardly were his university classes over for the summer, but that he and Daphna set off for two weeks in Rome, the kind of "in your face" romantic interlude Sarah Yogev attempted to mitigate the effects of upon her jilted and fragile older son by taking him, along with her husband and their younger daughter, on a two-week vacation to Provence. A friend of theirs, an Israeli politician of some note, had recently purchased a marvelous mansion there, on a cliff directly overlooking the Mediterranean. At the very least, Sarah thought, she could offer her sensitive older son something "poetic" to offset the more fleshly pleasures his younger brother was so obliviously occupied with in Rome.

As for Daphna Flinker, the weeks in Rome with her young lover—and without the burden of her three children, whom she had left with their grieving father—were a welcome reprieve from the life she had, it seemed, so eagerly abandoned. They, of course, visited the Coliseum and the Pantheon; kissed in front of the Trevi Fountain; strolled among the labyrinthine alleys of Trastevere, and amused themselves at the rows upon rows of washing strung out from the apartments in Mama-Leone tradition. They picnicked in the Roman Forum, and, after making a compulsory donation to the monks who guarded it, discretely made love in the Capuchin cemetery. It hardly bothered them when their landlady, a former Benedictine nun who, they detected from the outset, looked disapprovingly upon what she accurately perceived as their difference in age, finally threw them out, finding the late-night sounds of their lovemaking a bit too much for her and her ailing husband to take.

Luckily for the young couple, there was a vacant—and, given their limited budget, inexpensively priced—room available at the Hungarian Academy in Rome, in the very precious *Palazzo Falconieri* at via Giulia 1, where a friend of Peter Vajda's, a Hungarian-Israeli painter by the name of Sinai Sulzberger, had recently become Director. This allowed the young lovers to roam the very same corridors where such eminent Hungarians as the expert of Greek mythology, Károly Kerényi, the philosopher György Lukacs, the writer Antal Szerb, the poet Sándor Weöres, and the composer Zoltán Kodály—some of them even Jews!—

had once walked. So that their second week—with those around them seeming to revel in, rather than being disconcerted by, the late-night arias of Daphna Flinker—passed even more happily than had the first.

Simon's older brother, meanwhile, was enjoying the French coast and its many visual and culinary pleasures, and—surrounded by friends and family—his thoughts returned only infrequently to his former girlfriend. There were, after all, poems to be written, paintings to be made. The pleasures of the flesh had been intense, but brief. Nonetheless, a wound had opened within him—perhaps more a wound of repudiation than of loss, more one of wounded pride than of lost pleasure. For once, he had briefly triumphed over his younger brother—and, what's more, on the amorous battlefield where his brother had reigned so supreme! But now, that, too, was lost, and he was forced to reassume his previous persona as the bedazzled genius who cared little for earthly pleasures.

The family returned from their Provençal journey, and the young lovers from their romantic two weeks in Rome, at virtually the same time, so that the Yogevs and what had by now become their "extended" family—including not only Daphna, but her three children, somewhat reluctantly repossessed from their increasingly depressed father—once again reconvened at Galilee for what had now unofficially become the "anniversary" of Daphna Flinker's quasi-conjugal entry into the family circle—or, it might be more accurately stated, the family's entry into hers.

Unlike the previous year, it had been a torridly hot summer, even for the Middle East, the Galilee being no exception, and some of the obvious tension that had by now more or less solidified between the two brothers was slightly dissipated by periodic sojourns to the lake for refreshment—mostly in groups of two or three, with the two young lovers, of course, usually choosing to bicycle on their own, leaving the children in the care of Sarah Yogev or her young daughter Katya, who, at the age of twelve, had already developed something of a maternal instinct. Few, if any, words were exchanged between the brothers, while their mother did her utmost to constantly extol the enormous pleasures of their trip to France, thereby hoping to assure that the ever-turning wheels of jealousy and envy would be lubricated in the other direction as well.

On the eve of the holiday itself, ever hopeful of some reconciliation between the brothers and of reestablishing an atmosphere of family harmony, Sarah Yogev proposed that they all go to nearby Tiberias for a staged Hebrew-language performance of *The Tragedy of Man*, the dramatic poem by the famed nineteenth-century Hungarian Imre Madach that had often evoked comparison's to Milton's *Paradise Lost*. With the exception of David Yogev, who opted to stay home and work on his newly commissioned bust of Yitzhak Rabin, and Daphna, who felt uncomfortable about leaving the children in the care of someone who entered all too easily into a state of artistic trance, the others reluctantly agreed. Neither of the boys wanted to further disappoint their mother, who had seemed more than a bit edgy and depressed of late.

Not that the Madach play—Etan, himself hardly in an elevated mood, thought to himself—was a particularly uplifting choice of entertainment. Taking place after Adam and Eve's banishment from the Garden of Eden, in it Adam dreams the course of modern history, which only serves to fill him with despair. He, Eve, and Lucifer then take on different historical roles as they pass through ancient Rome, the Crusades, Kepler's Prague, revolutionary Paris, and finally, a post-historical time when ecological disaster has nearly destroyed the world.

Once he has learned of the degradation that awaits humanity, Adam considers suicide, but when he discovers Eve is pregnant, places his faith in God and the future. In all the play's scenes and anticipatory dreams, Adam, Eve, and the archfiend Lucifer are the chief and constantly recurring *personae dramatis*. As the play nears its end, Adam, despairing of his race, tries to commit suicide. But, at the critical moment Eve informs him that she is about to be a mother, and the play ends with Adam lying prostrate before God, who encourages him to hope and trust.

Etan had read the play several times—Simon, in fact, had read it as well, (albeit reluctantly; it had been assigned in his Central European Literature class) and looked upon the evening ahead with a dour countenance and a sagging spirit. But, he thought to himself, after all the obvious pain he had caused his mother and brother, going along was the very least he could do. What, after all, was a mere wasted evening in the greater scheme of things?

It was in this manner that Daphna Flinker and David Yogev, after Daphna had put the children to bed, found themselves alone in the Yogev's large kitchen later that evening, enjoying a quiet supper of Norwegian salmon, potato kugel, and green beans, expertly prepared in advance by Sarah, and a fine bottle of Gewurztraminer from the nearby Golan Heights Winery, owned by a friend of David's who had made his fortune in South African diamonds.

Daphna had always found David Yogev, even at seventy-two, an intriguing man. There was something terribly dignified about him, so cavalier, so—how else could she put it?—*Old Worldly*. He seemed to her like an aging Don Juan, a slightly pot-bellied Casanova, of times past. Lord Byron, had he lived to an old age, might well have come to resemble him.

"L'chaim," the older man toasted, clicking his glass against hers.

"L'chaim," she replied, smiling. He was certainly still an attractive man—the kind of man who, no matter how advanced his age, still adored women—but now, against the candlelight alone with his older son's paintings everywhere around them—he seemed even more attractive, even more diabolically cunning and wise.

There was much a woman could learn from older men, she had always been told, and he, no doubt, had already taught his share of younger women a great deal. Suddenly, she could feel her feet moving against his beneath the table. She could feel the pillows moving beneath her head once more. He was gazing, paternally yet seductively, into her eyes from across the table. Slowly but surely, he could feel her body, almost of its own accord, begin to rise, slowly heading toward yet another bed.

SHE AND I

She is quintessentially French. I am, in the loosest sense of the word, American. She always feels cold. I am always hot. In the winter, even if it isn't chilly, she does nothing but complain about how cold it is. Even in late spring, there are large, fertile fields of goose bumps on her thin, beautiful arms, and I have known her, even in the Middle East in late June, to wear a woolen sweater around the house, to sleep in a lamb's wool camisole in August.

She speaks, since she doesn't speak much, only one language well, though she seems to understand so much more than I do, even in the languages she doesn't really speak. I, on the other hand, can make myself understood in several languages, yet have trouble focusing on the conversations of others.

She enjoys reading maps and navigating around in new places. I hate it, and quickly grow impatient and ornery. After a single afternoon in a foreign city, she will have mastered the public transportation system, be able to find her way to the centrum from the most desolate-seeming corners. I will get lost five meters from my own hotel, or—worse yet—a new apartment. She hates asking for directions, preferring to gaze patiently at a to-me-indecipherable map for many moments. When we get lost, I am quick to blame her. She blames no one, but busies herself looking for second-hand shops and fruit and vegetable markets in whatever neighborhood we are lost in.

She loves old architecture, curved surfaces, rummaging among the trinkets and memorabilia of other people's lives at flea markets, the scent of flowers and herbs. I am always impatient to get where I'm going, missing virtually everything along the way. The only two things I've ever been able to love completely and unconditionally are my own disfigured face in the mirror and sitting at my desk making a kind of music exclusively with words . . . though I love my son, and sometimes her, in a different way, as well.

She loves travel, unfamiliar places, a sense of the unexpected. I dream of living always in one place, burning my passport, etching an address in stone upon my door post, running for mayor in some town I will never again move from.

I love to eat in restaurants—bad restaurants, good restaurants, even mediocre ones. She always wants to eat at home: fresh vegetables and better food, she claims, at a third the price. She hates the way I do the dishes and leave a mess after cooking. I like, on occasion, to do the dishes and cook, though I'm quite awful at the former, which I always do in too great a hurry, leaving all sorts of prints, smudges, and grease stains along the way.

She loves to watch a late movie—preferably a slow-moving, melancholic one of the French or Italian sort—and to have a glass of wine or two with dinner. I prefer rather superficial, fast-moving American films, fall asleep almost the second I enter the theatre for anything later than the 7:30 showing, and can drink, at most, a glass of white zinfandel in late afternoon.

She has little patience for, or interest in, pleasantries among strangers, preferring to restrict her circle of acquaintances to those she is truly intimate with. I enjoy talking to the garbage collector, the mailman, making small talk with the meter-reader and taxi driver. The greetings "How are you?" and "Have a nice day" do not cause me to rail against the superficiality of America and Americans.

She is shy; I am not. Occasionally, however, her shyness rubs off on me, or, alternatively—as in the case of landlords who are trying to take advantage of us or rabbis who are too adamantly in favor of circumcision—she loses her shyness and grows quite eloquent, even in English, her vocabulary suddenly expanding to include words like *barbaric* and *philistine*.

She has no respect for established authority, and thinks nothing of running out on student loans, disconnecting the electric meter, or not paying taxes. I, on the other hand, though I have the face of an anarchist, am afraid of established authority and tend, against my own better instincts, to respect it. As soon as I spot a police car in the rearview mirror, I assume I have done something terribly wrong and begin to contemplate spending the rest of my life in jail. She, on the other hand, smiles shyly at the police officer, who quickly folds up his notebook and goes back to his car.

She likes goat's cheese, garlic, a good slice of pâté with a glass of red wine, tomatoes with fresh rosemary. I like sausages, raw meat, pizza, and gefilte fish with very sharp horseradish.

She claims that I am a Neanderthal when it comes to food, a barbaric American animal who will die young of high cholesterol, rancid oils, and pesticides. She is refined, has a sensitive palate and a nose so accurate it can tell the difference between day-old and two-day-old butter. When we lived in Cambridge, Massachusetts, she spent many days in search of the perfect, vine-ripened tomato and just the right kind of basil for making pesto. She can't stand, for example, pine nuts that are rancid. "Rancid," in fact, is one of the English words she uses most frequently.

At the cinema she hates to sit too close to the screen, and—if we're at home—refuses to watch movies on TV that are interrupted by commercials, claiming that it interferes with her "dream world." I like to sit near the front of the theatre and tell jokes during the movie. I like almost any movie, as long as it is superficial enough not to disturb my worldview. She prefers dark, slow-moving, romantic tragedies, set to the music of Jacques Brel, which linger in her imagination for many days after, causing her to question, or reexamine, almost everything in her world. She remembers the names of films and actors, and prefers actresses who embody a kind of low-key sensuality and dark reserve. I adore those who are brazenly sexual and whore-like in their demeanor. If, for example, as in Roman Polanski's *Bitter Moon*, there are two women, one of whom is subtly beautiful, sensual, and slightly tragic, the other who is vulgar, brazen, hedonistic, and rather shallow, it is always certain that she will prefer the first. I always prefer the second.

On those rare occasions when we've seen a film we both liked, she will, the next day—even the next month—remember every small detail of it: the weather in a particular scene, the shape of an awning, the way a blouse or a cloth napkin lay against the protagonist's arm or lap. I, on the other hand, will remember nothing, not even the plot, as if some premature and obliterating dementia had overtaken me during the night. Somewhat sheep-faced, I will ask her to remind me what the movie was about, who was in it . . . on occasion, even, what it's name was, all of which she will generously do, never even pausing to comment upon my infirmity.

Though I am rather smart about books and literature, it is the rare film in which I am even able to follow the plot line, much less unravel the mystery, so that, after we leave the theatre (assuming I haven't fallen asleep), I will usually need her to explain to me exactly what happened, who was related to whom, and why, at the end, a photograph of one character's daughter mysteriously showed up on the wall of a seemingly unrelated character's living room. When she does, I am inevitably embarrassed about my simple-mindedness and lack of insight, a shortcoming she seems either oblivious to or willing to overlook.

I either love or hate people, and find myself utterly incapable of having any interest in those I am indifferent to. She, though often equally indifferent to the same people, always seeks to find something interesting and unique about them, a pursuit I have neither the time nor patience for. Something in even the most uninspiring person arouses, if not her conversation, then at least her curiosity, and—once she has been engaged with someone in any way—she retains a certain ongoing loyalty to them I can neither relate to or comprehend. Though far less extroverted than I am, she will carry on a correspondence with any number of people, in all sorts of countries, and keeps a list in her address book of all the birthdays of everyone she has ever known and liked.

I consider every crisis a catastrophe, and will begin to fidget nervously and despondently whenever I am confronted with a late train, a rescheduled flight, or an incompetent waitperson. She considers each of these events a hidden opportunity, a portent from the gods, yet another manifestation of the world's independence and revivifying fickleness.

Though I have somehow been appointed the "breadwinner" of our family, I am extremely lazy: my favorite activity, as Freud said of poets, is daydreaming, my buttocks wedged firmly in a chair. She is never idle, raising domesticity to an art form, a Buddhist perfection in every ironed crease.

Being a devotee of Bishop Berkeley's formulation to the effect that, if you can't see it, it isn't there, I prefer neatness to cleanliness: My idea of housecleaning is to sweep the large dust balls under the bed, stuff plastic and paper bags sloppily into a kitchen cabinet, cover the bed hurriedly with a creased down comforter, cram my underwear (freely mingling with socks) into a dresser drawer. She is almost maniacally clean, sniffing each of my shirts and socks daily to make sure they don't need to be washed, vacuuming in corners, changing the pillowcases and sheets with the regularity of tides.

I like to buy cheap things, particularly clothes, frequently, wearing them until they fray or lose their shape, and then cart them from place to place without ever wearing them again. One of the things she seems to enjoy most is to go through my clothes closets, reminding me of all the cheap items I bought and never wore, or which I have worn once, washed, and which are now "totally useless." She buys clothes almost never, but always things of good quality, preferring to wear the same few things (always immaculately clean) time and time again.

I fancy myself a great dancer and a sex object. She thinks of herself as physically awkward and more sensual than sexy. I can type like a madman and, albeit reluctantly, use a computer. She considers a keyboard a frightful artifact.

I like to drive. She likes to navigate. On those few occasions on which she drives our car, I nag her relentlessly about shifting at the wrong speeds, or squeezing too hard on the brakes. When she navigates and we begin to lose our way, I immediately become so ornery and hostile that, on at least one occasion in Budapest, she threatened to get out of the car and go home on her own. In countries known for their dangerous drivers, she insists I do all the driving, an affirmation of my manhood I accept reluctantly, though I don't object to being in control.

I am the kind of person who can do many things at once, most of them rather imperfectly. She does only one thing at a time, but always with a sense of perfection.

I like to cook without recipes, freely mixing Marsala wine, mustard, artichoke hearts, candied ginger, maple syrup, and plums, hoping something capable of being digested will emerge. She always uses a recipe—except for things she has made before—but everything she makes is successful and delicious.

I would have been a rock star, or a concert pianist—or perhaps, even, the proprietor of an illicit sex club—had I felt freer to follow my lyrical and immoral heart's calling. She would have been a sister in a Carmelite Monastery, or a gardener.

She is an enthusiastic and natural mother. I am a reluctant father.

She could have been many things, all of them having something to do with taking care of others or using her hands: a nurse, a dentist, a carpenter, a potter, a refinisher of furniture, a restorer of antiquarian books. I could, though I like to imagine otherwise, probably have done only the one thing I am doing now: putting words to paper.

I like to live part of my life in the if-but-only mode of wishful thinking and fantastical alternatives. She accepts the life life has given her as her one possible destiny, without complaining.

She doesn't like to think of money—in fact, her refusal to think about it has, on occasion, gotten her (and me!) into heaps of trouble. I, while I don't like to think of it either, am usually left with the unpoetic task of having to worry about it. Since I have been with her, in fact, hardly a day has passed without thinking of it . . . almost constantly. She, on the other hand, worries about many other unpoetic tasks in our lives that have nothing at all to do with money.

I can imitate people from many countries, and with many different accents. She is too much herself to imitate anyone.

I like to have some kind of music playing whenever I am not reading or working. She usually prefers silence, or only to have music on when she is actually listening to it.

I will continue to eat even when I am no longer hungry, just for the pleasure of it. She eats only as much as satisfies her hunger on any occasion. I abhor all forms of table manners, eating with my fingers, chewing with my mouth open, taking food freely from others' plates, licking my fingers at the table, stuffing my mouth with large quantities, burping and passing gas. She never eats before being seated at the table, waits for everyone else to do likewise, chews only small morsels at a time, and eats so slowly, and with such deliberate pleasure, that I have usually finished what is on my plate well before she is actually seated. Only twice in our eight years together have I observed her passing gas. Burping, never.

As soon as I make a decision, I immediately, and relentlessly, tilt toward wanting the other alternative. She immediately accepts, and begins to implement, any decision she has made. She often says that I am a neurotic and "special" kind of person; she feels that, living with me, this kind of behavior is the "statue quo." Occasionally, when I am in one of my periods of manic reconsideration, she smiles slightly in her slightly smiling French way, as if to say, "*Oy vey*, what a case I am married to."

I like to eat on the street—frequently, and mostly greasy and unhealthy foods—which accounts for the fact that most of my clothing have grease and/or coffee stains on them, souvenirs of my animalistic habits she claims American washing machines are incapable of eradicating. Most of all, I like to devour greasy Hungarian sausages at stand-up counters in Budapest. She likes to eat only "à table," quietly, savoring every morsel of, say, pâté with, preferably, a glass of red wine. Among the tastes in life I can truly not abide are *pasteque,* fennel, and every form of anise, all of which she has rather an affection for.

I am often angry at others, friends, foes, and family alike, and like to hold, and nurse, these angers for as long as is humanly possible, until I can almost feel them eating at my liver, like an earthquake with numerous, sustained aftershocks. She is incapable of sustained anger or hostility and would, I believe, (perhaps already has) forgive me the most egregious deeds and betrayals, an attitude I have no desire to test to its limits. Even in her case, I like to remind her as often as possible of the ways she has disappointed and betrayed me. She, on the other hand, rarely mentions my betrayals and weaknesses.

I never cry, even when I am truly unhappy, yet I have a tendency to grow teary-eyed whenever an athlete experiences some major triumph, or after the last out of the World Series, when the players all rush to the mound and hug each other. She cries easily, even at sentimental movies whose pandering to sentimental feelings she despises.

I will take any kind of pill or medicine anyone recommends in order to relieve pain and discomfort. She prefers "natural" remedies. Although I am not terribly Jewish by religious conviction, I wanted to have our son circumcised when he was born. She felt it to be a pagan ritual tantamount to permanent disfigurement, and began assembling propaganda from various anti-circumcision organizations around the country depicting vast armadas of mutilated children with heavily bandaged penises. She won. She usually wins.

I think she is beautiful, but too thin, and am constantly after her to try and gain weight. She thinks she is less beautiful than I do, but comments frequently about her "beautiful arms." When she was younger, in California, she wore her hair very short and looked like a kind of postmodern French punktress on her way to the wrong discotheque. Now, I think, she is much more beautiful and womanly, and, like I am, a bit older.

When we met in Ecuador, she had rather gray hair and was wearing purple nylon pants and a yellow sweatshirt. She seemed, at first, more interested in reading her mail than in talking to me, a fact that I soon realized was due more to her shyness—and her passion for her mail—than to lack of interest in me. On the two-hour bus ride between Quito and Otavalo, across the Equator, I slowly began to realize that she was quite beautiful, in an undemonstrative sort of way, and that night, as I way of getting myself into her room and closer to her bed in the hotel where she, her female traveling companion and I were staying, I planned to borrow her toothpaste. But she wasn't, I discovered, as shy as she seemed, and it turned out I didn't need to do that. The next morning I remember her companion bringing two glasses of fresh-squeezed orange juice to the room, along with coffee, and then our walking, hand in hand, above the town of Otavalo, where we finally sat in a small restaurant and her friend Annick took our picture. I looked very happy in the photo, though not too handsome. She looked happy too, and quite lovely.

We stayed in several very lovely, and inexpensive, small

Ecuadorian hotels during those days, and I remember, not even a week after not having to borrow her toothpaste, looking down at her one night (or was it afternoon?) and saying, "I think I love you." "I think I love you too, Gringo," she replied. She used to call me "Gringo" in those days.

I remember talking to her an awful lot back then, and thinking to myself how attentively, and compassionately, she always listened. I myself am not such a good listener, except on occasion, so that—along with the sweet way she always said "uh huh, uh huh . . ." and "yes . . . yes" when I was telling her a story—it made a real impression on me. Back then, I don't remember her being nearly as cold, or quite as thin . . . but, then again, we were in love and in Ecuador.

Sometimes, now, when I realize we have been together for more than eight years and have a seven-year-old son, I think that this is one of the major miracles of my life . . . and I'm sure she does also. I was so romantic then, that night in Otavalo, and so was she when, hardly a week later, she got on a plane from Quito to the United States and followed me to Boston. I remember her calling me, as we had planned, but suddenly having a sense that the call wasn't quite long distance. When she told me she was standing at a pay telephone across the street at Porter Square, I ran down the stairs, not even bothering to button my shirt or pull up my zipper, and took her into my arms and carried her halfway up to my fourth-floor, rent-controlled apartment.

I was stronger in those days, and healthier, and so, maybe, was she. We were not so young, but very much in love, and there was a scent of laundry, somehow, wafting through my windows as we made love, on a mattress located on my study floor, for the first time in the United States of America.

Now, as I write this, I am sitting in Israel, and we will

soon be in Paris, then in Provence, and then back in the United States of America, the only country whose language I have truly mastered. I no longer live in that rent-controlled apartment and that mattress, I am quite sure, is no longer on the floor. She is still beautiful, though—perhaps even more so—with her knowing eyes and beautiful smile and lovely French voice, and she is still, as a friend of mine once described her, *"une chouette"*: an owl.

THE DEATH OF FEKETE

When Aunt Etus's son's dog, Bori, bit Kormány Lajos in his right leg at the vineyards of Szent György Hill, it seemed only logical to the bored and unemployed men of the village—Gyula, Roland, Feri, and Kormány himself—that the dog had to be shot.

Because Etus's son, Árpi, was a large man, however, known to have a bad temper, especially when drunk, self-preservation dictated a wiser course: namely, to shoot Etus's small puli, Fekete, instead. So the four men, after borrowing Uncle Dönci's old Hungarian World War I police rifle, grabbed the "innocent looking dog from Etus's front yard" by the ears, bound him into an oversized potato sack, and took him up into the back of Gyula's winemaking house, where they fired a round of six cartridges into the helpless animal, who yelped and twitched when the first bullet entered his abdomen, and then moved no more.

The dog, to be sure, was quite dead after the shooting, and it seemed to many a gratuitous bit of cruelty when the body, blown into small bits, was left on Etus's doorstep. Though everyone in the village realized that Kormány had been involved, blame for the heinous event somehow began to center around the illiterate and partially deaf Feri, who had, for years, been spending his days, from late morning to well after midnight, ensconced at the local pub, and whose appetite for cheap *pálinka* followed by large glasses of Balaton *Olaszrizling* was as extensive as his vocabulary was small.

It was not that Feri was considered cruel: he was universally acknowledged, rather, to be simply stupid, and like most stupid men, easily prone to the role of follower. Moreover, it had long been suspected that Roland and Gyula, the more robust and mischievous of the unemployed quartet, exerted an undue influence over the hapless lad, who—much to Kormány's embarrassment—was a distant cousin of his as well. Feri's mental infirmities, it had been suspected, were the logical by-product of the too frequent marriages and procreations among cousins and near-cousins that village life inevitably spawned.

In many ways the most innocent of the foursome, Feri spent his increasingly scarce hours away from the pub collecting, and meticulously inventorying, old Elvis Presley and Beatles albums, the one mental activity his limited intelligence could apparently master. Always dressed, no matter how hot or dry the season, in tattered brown leather overalls, a pair of green, knee-high rubber boots known as *gumi csizma*, a black-and-red woolen ski cap that looked as if it had originally been skied in during the reign of Kaiser Franz Joseph, and a New York Yankees baseball cap, he was known—for the village's annual Szent Lőrinc Festival dance following the soccer match between Hegymagas and neighboring Káptalantóti—to treat himself to a much-welcomed shower and shave, after which he would don the dark gray wool suit that had once been his father's.

Feri senior, the former village postmaster, had been run over by a mule-drawn Gypsy cart ten years earlier while staggering home from his mistress's house in neighboring Raposka. His father's death and the suicide of his retarded younger sister, which followed almost immediately upon it, had driven the boy (everyone referred to him as "the boy," though he was nearly forty) only deeper into the inertia of village life, so that he was now as much a fixture on the wooden bench outside the *Italbolt* as was the pub's bench itself, rousing himself into action only when some sort of entertainment—such as the soccer match or, everyone now speculated, the shooting of Etus's dog—was offered in its place.

The bite on Kormány Lajos's leg, in fact, had been a bad one, and it was the universal sentiment that Kormány—a frequent trespasser on, and pilferer from, the largely unoccupied vineyard houses—had probably trespassed one too many times on Árpi's three grape-filled hectares, thus becoming the object of Bori's, and his master's, proprietary instincts.

Etus, on the other hand, was the best loved of the village's large group of widowed *nénis*, a woman of boundless generosity and good will who—in addition to being the traditional winner of the annual fish soup contest each August—was known to wander from house to house, distributing ears of corn and the small unsweetened round cakes known as *pogácsa* to the children and the bedridden, her tattered and (to the dismay of all who loved her) foul-smelling apron tied around her neck and a good word for everyone on her lips.

Etus had adopted Fekete several years earlier, when the dog followed her home on her bicycle from the market in Tapolca. She could still ride long distances in those days, and the two of them had been virtually inseparable ever since, the dog following loyally at Etus's feet as she made her way from the vineyard to the pub on her various missions of mercy. Fekete, a small, affectionate, though somewhat yappy animal, was hardly prone to outbreaks of aggressiveness unless severely provoked or, it turned out, finding itself in Árpi's immediate vicinity, where— much like his more formidable cousin Bori—he experienced a kind of transformation of personality consonant with Árpi's ornery and frequently inebriated ways.

On the day of the incident that led to Fekete's death, Kormány, having downed one too many *pálinkas* for breakfast, had apparently wandered onto the perimeters of Árpi's vineyard as he set off into the hills. The two men had had a history of altercations, large and small, dating back some ten years earlier when Kormány had sold Árpi a supposedly reconditioned Trabant station wagon for 20,000 forints, only to have the engine utter its last gasp before its new owner could even make it to Tapolca for a new front fender.

On the morning in question Árpi, suffering from a headache and hangover, was not at all disappointed to see Kormány staggering toward him and eagerly sent Bori, chomping at the bit, off in the trespasser's direction. It was only seconds later that a howl reverberated throughout the vineyards, as the dog's sharp canine teeth tore through Kormány's three-generation-old overalls and nestled in his right leg, penetrating all the way through the flesh and into the fibula.

Kormány's wife, a nurse in the local hospital, seemed to take a certain private glee in her husband's injury. Nonetheless, she was reluctantly summoned to bandage the wound and check the dog for rabies, her negative verdict concerning which did little to alleviate either Kormány's anger, or his pain.

Kormány, in fact, had never been terribly fond of Etus, having long felt that her virtual lock on the annual fish soup prize was one of the reasons for his own mother's premature death from a cardiac infarction—he described it as a "fish-soup-broken heart"—two years earlier. The elder Aunt Kormány's concoction, her son knew, had been *far* superior to Etus's soup, and it was only the sentimental admiration in which Etus and her family were held—as contrasted with the distance most of the villagers kept from the legendarily drunken Kormány clan—that, he was certain, explained such an undeserved monopoly.

Gyula, the eldest of the foursome, had once made what seemed a reasonable living as a go-between in the summer rental market for vineyard houses to Austrian tourists. But he had fallen victim, both to his increasing penchant for women and drink, and his inability to accommodate his rather lackadaisical spirit to the realities of the new market economy. Each passing year found him spending more and more of his time at the *Italbolt* in the company of Roland, a former carpenter who had severed his right hand with a chainsaw while drunk three years earlier, and less and less time at the "business office"—a three-legged kitchen table supported by bricks, on top of which was perched a 1928 maroon Continental typewriter—he had set up in his widowed mother's pantry.

So—when news of Kormány Lajos's wounding spread from the vineyard to the ABC store, and then from the ABC store to the pub—it took little in the way of urging for the wounded victim to recruit Gyula and Roland to the righteousness of his quest for vengeance against relatively affluent, and well-respected, Etus and her clan.

Etus herself, who spent much of her time baking cheese strudel to be sold at the beach in nearby Szigliget, was hardly a vindictive sort, and—wounded as she was by the violent death of her beloved puli—would have preferred to let the incident pass and get on with her acts of charity and culinary generosity. Nor was Árpi, whose drinking and carousing Etus was convinced had caused the premature death of his father some twenty years earlier, easily aroused from his usual, less than fully conscious, state on his mother's behalf.

But the writer Fischer and the sculptor, Kepes, both of whose families had been longtime friends of Etus's, felt particularly aggrieved by Fekete's death and the consigning of Etus to a kind of second widowhood. The day after the killing, they took it upon themselves to pay a visit to the Mayor, Horvath János, to inquire as to what justice could be rendered the cold-blooded killers of Etus's dog.

Horvath János was a firm believer in maintaining the village's veneer of tranquility at all costs. He had for years been witness to the "revolving door" of trying to tame the impulses of the troublesome quartet—periodic short-term jailings in nearby Tapolca, accompanied by repeated reprimands by both himself and the local police chief—none of which had resulted in even the slightest change in their behavior.

"Kedves barátaim," he addressed Fischer and Kepes as he invited them into his winemaking house on Szent György hill. "My dear friends…There is really nothing I can do about this matter. It is, after all, only a *dog*, and not a human being, that has been put to death."

"Yes, of course, it's a dog," Fischer, not one to be easily intimidated, replied, "but it's a *widow's* dog—a widow, I might add, who has been a source of kindness in this village for more than sixty years—and I don't think we should merely stand by and do nothing when poor Etus's companion—an innocent dog, at that—is murdered in cold blood by four no-good drunkards."

"I agree," Kepes, who rarely left the confines of his newly converted studio, even to go to the Lake, and had been dragged along by Fischer, concurred. "It is not good for the village's reputation," he added, appealing to an area he knew to be high on the list of the Mayor's concerns, "for the dogs of our widows to be randomly slaughtered."

Kepes's appeal to Hegymagas's public relations seemed to have a momentary impact on the Mayor, who paused to remove the glass *borlopó* he had been using to fill a bottle of Chardonnay from a wooden cask from his lips.

"Yes," he said, "I suppose you're right—it's not good for the village's image. But, on the other hand, we must remember," he was quick to add, immediately returning to his avocation, "that we are not Keszthely . . . it is hardly as if *droves* of German and Austrian tourists in search of cheap dental care will be discouraged from coming here by the death of a dog. Why, we don't even *have* a dentist!"

"I am *not* talking about public relations," Fischer, a former *samizdat* writer and democratic resistance leader who was quick to lapse into cosmopolitan-style abstractions, was turning rather red. "I am talking about *justice* for poor Etus and her dog."

The Mayor, a member of the rather right-wing Smallholder's Party that was currently part of the governing coalition, had never been terribly fond of Fischer. He looked up from his more domestic duties, removing the *borlopó* once again from between his lips.

"Kedves barátom," he said, addressing the writer with a combination of feigned respect and ill-disguised disdain, "I am afraid that such appeals to higher authorities carry far more weight in Budapest than here in our little village. I am merely trying, as best I can, to keep the peace."

A slight expression of distaste began to make its way onto Fischer's face as he paused to take a sip of the Mayor's rather mediocre Sauvignon Blanc. "It is not," he replied, "a 'higher authority' we are appealing to . . . it is *your* authority."

"And *that* authority, I am afraid, *kedves Fischer úr,"* the Mayor rejoined, "is severely limited by the realities of our village life."

Disgusted by what he perceived to be the Mayor's condescending and parochial, small-town attitude, Fischer, followed obediently by Kepes, turned on his heels and strode out the door of the Mayor's cottage. "In that case," he turned to address the Mayor once more as the twosome headed back down the hill, "we will simply have to take justice for poor Etus into our own hands."

***

Hardly three days later, Kormány Lajos's prize sheep, a dark-haired animal by the name of Levente, was found hanging from a large oak just behind the stream that separated the village from neighboring Raposka.

The very next day, one of Hegymagas's most eloquent citizens, the thirty-four-year-old parrot, Attila, was found dead on the floor of his wooden cage beside the kitchen table in Gyula's mother's kitchen. Not even the most loving ministrations of Kormány Lajos's wife could revive the bird—a gift from Gyula's grandmother shortly after her emigration to Chile in 1956—who had startled, and endeared itself to, even Hegymagas's most patriotic citizens with its ability to pronounce the nearly unpronounceable Hungarian word for drugstore—*gyógyszertár.*

But it was only when, finally, Feri's antique *gumi csizma* were found, the following week, melted into a foul-smelling rubbery blob in the stone fireplace just below Árpi's hillside hectares, and Roland's prosthetic hand was discovered, the following day, to have been stolen from his bedside table, that the Mayor decided the time had come to involve himself personally in the increasingly anarchic system of law and order that was threatening to engulf the village.

Knocking on the door of Fischer's two-story village house late one afternoon, Horvath, emboldened by a half bottle of plum *pálinka*, greeted the writer with the habitual Hungarian kiss on each cheek.

"Jó napot kivánok, kedves barátaim," the Mayor announced, stepping over the threshold into the kitchen and adopting what was, *vis à vis* Fischer, an unusually amiable tone. "Good day."

"Good day, *kedves Polgármester úr,"* Fischer sensed that something had gone a bit awry, and responded politely but guardedly. "Come in and have a seat."

The Mayor, deciding to take advantage of the momentary air of conviviality that had entered his relationship with Fischer, cut right to the heart of the matter.

"It seems," he said, exhaling deeply and moving to light a cigarette, "that certain citizens of our village have decided to take justice into their own hands with regard Etus *néni's* dog . . . And I am not," he continued before Fischer could get a word in by way of response, "very happy about it."

Fischer was just about to undergo a radical change of mood and tear into the Mayor concerning his unhappiness with the Hegymagasian system of justice, when there was a knock on the door and Etus herself entered the Fischer's kitchen. Beneath her right arm were six ears of freshly cut corn and, in her left hand, a plastic bag containing several dozen assorted plain and cheese *pogácsák*.

"Kedves Polgármester," she gave the Mayor a kiss on

both cheeks. *"Kedves barátaim,"* she likewise greeted Fischer, simultaneously mouthing the Hungarian words for good day. *"Jó napot kivánok."*

"How lovely to see you, Etus *néni,"* Fischer, ever the gentleman among women, softly kissed his elderly neighbor's hand. *"Kezit csókolom."*

"I am not good," Etus, placing her two loads on the Pilinskzys' kitchen table, replied. "Not good at all." To Fischer's surprise, and the Mayor's embarrassment, a small flotilla of tears suddenly began tumbling down Etus's cheeks.

"It is not right, what is happening in our small village, on account of my poor little Fekete, and I want for everyone—I repeat, *everyone*—to please stop behaving in this way, so that we can all live together again in peace."

No sooner had the word "peace" echoed into the room from poor Etus's lips, however, but a tremendous splattering of shattered glass could be heard coming from Fischer's backyard. Running out into the garden, tear-stricken Etus and her reeking apron just behind them, the Mayor and Fischer were confronted with the heartrending sight of Fischer's once-intact clerestory window scattered all over the lawn in a million glistening small fragments. Inside, nestled tranquilly between Fischer's hirsute begonias and his upturned prize oleander bush, was a large gray stone with the words *csunya disznók!*— ugly pigs!—painted on it in a pigment all too closely resembling pig's blood.

"Kedves Isten!" muttered Etus, tears still running down her cheek. "Dear God, what will we do now?"

"We do," Fischer, never one to linger without a solution, replied, "the only thing any civilized village would do—we drive the bastards out of town."

Fischer's reveries of prairie justice, however, were quickly interrupted by a terrible howling sound, like that of a dog with its leg caught in a trap, coming from somewhere across Széchenyi út, followed by the sound of rubber being left on the dusty street, as a car accelerated out of town.

"Now, what the hell is *that?*" the Mayor cried out, running out into the street, where he was met by the sight of a large pig—from all appearances, Árpi's pet pig Kadar—dragging its bloody, partially severed tail down the street and howling for all it was worth. Through the dusty aftermath of what had just taken place, the Mayor was fairly sure he could still make out the contours of a rusted yellow Trabant, exactly like Gyula's, leaving yet another patch of rubber on the road as it turned right and headed toward Tapolca.

***

An eerie, unnatural quiet permeated the village over the next several days—a quiet more characteristic of the short, wintry days of February than the busy tourist season of mid-July. Even the ABC store, site of the ritual daily lineup for fresh bread and cottage cheese, began to take on the lonely, abandoned feeling of an athletic stadium during the off-season. Etus, Terika néni and Vera néni, the three widows whose pained and stuttering promenades along Széchenyi út could be counted on to punctuate the monotony of village life, were nowhere to be seen, and—to the utter incredulity of all the village's 278 permanent residents—even Feri and his perpetually filled pitcher of Kaiser *sör* had disappeared from the bench in front of the *Italbolt*.

As for Kormány Lajos, whom everyone credited with being the body whose hand had catapulted the stone through Pinlinszky's window, neither he nor Gyula and Roland were anywhere to be seen. Rumors began to circulate that the foursome had stolen a car from the junkyard in nearby Szigliget and taken off for Transylvania. Nonetheless, fears that one or more of them, stones, blades or shotguns in hand, could resurface at any moment were more than enough to cast a melancholic pall over the village's usual summer rituals of pig roasts, bonfires, wine tastings and infidelities.

Several nights after the shattering of Fischer's window, Kepes, Fischer, the Mayor, and—at Etus's urging—Árpi were meeting at the now-deserted *Italbolt* to discuss what action might be taken to restore peace and tranquility to the Hegymagasian summer.

"We must," inveighed Kepes, "despite what has happened to our poor neighbor Fischer's window, and to Árpi's pig, allow an atmosphere of generosity and forgiveness to prevail."

"Yes," seconded the Mayor. "We are a small and peaceful village. We must love one another or die."

Fischer, still contemplating the replacement cost of his destroyed window and his unsalvageable oleander, remained silent for a rare moment, as if contemplating not merely his own destiny, but the world's future.

Árpi lifted a glass of plum pálinka skyward in a rather elegant arc, coming to a halt at his lips. "Yes," he agreed, making a slurping noise with his tongue and casting a lascivious eye toward Kati the bartender, "we should all kiss and make up . . . for my mother's sake if no one else's. And who knows?—Kadar's tail may yet grow back."

"Well," Fischer broke his silence with the reluctance of someone at an auction contemplating whether to bid far more than he had intended, "I'm not so sure. Peace and forgiveness have their place in the world, but so does justice. First it's poor Fekete, then my clerestory window, and now Kadar's tail. I, personally, have had more than my fill of those four bums and their troublemaking. Who knows *what* it will be next?

"It's about time," he continued, no doubt thinking about his own offspring, "that we set a better example for our children, and I see no reason why we shouldn't begin right here and now."

"It's not exactly as if the two of *you* have been standing passively by watching the whole thing from the sidelines," the Mayor reminded Fischer, taking on a rather scolding tone. "I think that Kormány's sheep, Gyula's parrot, Feri's gumicsizma and Roland's arm are a more than adequate display of village justice, don't you?"

"I'm not sure." Fischer seemed to be trying hard, at this point, to restrain a faint smile from trickling onto his lips. "I'm not at all sure."

***

Yet another week went by, with still no sign of the fabulous foursome, or, for that matter, of the village's usual spirit of lightheartedness and conviviality. Sipos Lajos, a carpenter from nearby Káptalantóti, was hard at work repairing Fischer's window, and Árpi and Kadar—the latter with a splint and massive bandage appended to its disfigured tail—kept a hesitant vigil up in the vineyard.

A resonant emptiness—punctuated, periodically, by a visit by Kepes and Fischer for a glass of Slivovitz—echoed from the *Italbolt*, and even the village's two garrulous Germans, Kronzucker and his wife Ulrike, seemed to have decided to curtail their weekly invitations for *Bratwurst und Hefeweise* at their backyard barbecue.

On this particularly torrid night, with a severe summer thunderstorm threatening, Horvath, Kepes, and Fischer were once again seated in the bar, a funereal pall having been cast over the former's attempts at peacemaking by the latter's intransigence and the other's relative apathy.

"I guess it's going to be a long, unfriendly summer," Kepes remarked, lighting one of his socialist-era Kossuth cigarettes. "A *very* long summer."

Suddenly, the front door of the *Italbolt* flew open, and in stumbled Feri, bootless and forlorn-seeming, his mud-strewn Yankee cap tilted to one side *à la* DiMaggio, a guitar with two broken strings grasped rather tentatively in his left hand. He was obviously drunk—more drunk, even, than usual—and, placing the guitar on one knee as he leaned backward against the ice cream freezer, began singing a bizarrely Hungarianized take on an old Peter, Paul, and Mary tune, now titled *"Hova lett a sok halászlé?"*—"Where has all the fish soup gone?"

"What a crazy sonuvabitch," Fischer muttered under his breath, lifting his beaker of Slivovitz to his lips.

"I think it's rather touching, in its own way," Kepes observed. "The poor boy is merely a creative spirit gone astray."

There was, however, on this particular occasion, a bit more to Feri's melancholic tune than mere drunken creativity. "Why don't you take a look outside, my friends," he interrupted his tune to suggest. Followed closely by Kepes, Fischer made his way to the *Italbolt* door, from where—gathered across the street on the Post Office lawn beneath a blackening sky—he observed an incredible sight: NO MORE COOKING UNTIL WE HAVE PEACE! The two men read out loud from the large cardboard placard being held up on the post office lawn by none other than Etus *néni,* Terika *néni,* Vera *néni,* Rosza *néni,* Zsuza *néni,* Anikó *néni* and Kati *néni*—in other words, by all seven of the village's surviving widows! The town's women, led by Vera *néni,* had apparently decided that—Hungarian morality traveling, as it did, through the lower regions of the body—they would try and put an end to the summer's hatreds and retributions by organizing a kind of culinary work stoppage.

"I don't believe it," Fischer turned incredulously to Kepes, who was unable to keep a hardly faint smile from trickling onto his lips. "Those crazy broads are actually organizing a *strike!*"

***

A strike, indeed, it turned out to be, as, over the next several days, the village's usually abundant supply of fish soup, *túrós rétes, paprikás csirke, mákos gombos, pörkölt, gulyás*, and *Hortobágyi palacsinta* virtually dried up. The men of the village found themselves increasingly dependent on the fare offered by the grease-laden and radically overpriced Szent György Pince, or the more reasonably priced, but quantitatively miniscule, offerings at Jóska Bácsi's new roadside restaurant, which simultaneously ran jeep tours of the vineyard, guided by the chef. Worse yet, many of them reverted to the sort of all-liquid diet that had already taken its toll on far too many Hungarians, both famous and infamous, in the past.

By the third day of the strike, Fischer was suffering from stomach cramps and diarrhea, Kepes's ulcer had been aggravated by an excess of alcohol, and even the Mayor, whose damaged pancreas dictated a diet at some remove from the Hungarian norm (which his wife, before going on strike, had lovingly supplied) began suffering from severe nausea and insomnia.

Feri himself, somehow inspired to new levels of eloquence and sobriety by the strike, began, oddly enough, serving as a kind of middleman between the village's peace-loving and newly undomesticated women and its disputatious men. "All they are saying," he informed Horvath and Fischer later that week at the *Italbolt*, borrowing a line from one of his heroes, "is give peace a chance."

Fischer, looking rather anemically pale, was cast into a state of profound reflection by Feri's borrowed words. "Well," he said, somehow forcing a conciliatory expression onto his features, "perhaps they have a point . . . This *is* getting to be a rather unpleasant summer, after all." With the exception of the *Italbolt*'s proprietress, Kati, for whose business the conflict had proved an unexpected boon, all the other patrons, overhearing the conversation from their usual positions hunched over a pálinka, broke into applause. *"Kössünk békét!"* cried out Tibor the dairy farmer, "Let's make peace!"

The Mayor, lifting his Slivovitz into the air, beamed with the air of a politician who had just brokered an agreement in the Middle East. "Then it's decided," he said. "We'll have peace." Fischer, following almost enthusiastically in his example, lifted his glass into the air. *"Egészségedre . . .* to Hegymagas!"

The next morning, a Saturday, an even stranger gathering than the previous day's found itself amassed on the Post Office lawn. Feri, freshly shaven and showered and wearing his gray suit beneath his New York Yankees baseball cap, was seated on a high stool, guitar in lap. To either side of him, were standing Árpi and Etus, the latter in a freshly washed and ironed apron. Behind them were gathered some two dozen of the village's children and, at the very rear—wearing somewhat alcohol-induced, but nonetheless genuinely amiable smiles—were Gyula, Roland, and, dressed in his Sunday best, Kormány.

At the sight of Fischer, Kepes, and the Mayor walking toward them down Széchenyi út, the gathered group, led by Feri's rather arrhythmic strumming on the guitar, burst into song.

"All we are saaaaying," the Hegymagasians sang in an English that would surely have made John Lennon wince in his grave, *"is give peace a chance."*

"All we are saaaaying," Etus, perpetually a good half-beat behind, intoned along, just as the sky opened and a torrential but soothing rain began to fall, *"is give peace a chance."*

***

Hardly forty-eight hours later, Gyula's mother awoke to the sound of a bird squawking *"jó reggelt kivánok"*—"Good morning"—loudly in Hungarian. She went outside to find a brand new parrot, in a filigreed wooden cage, mounted on a stand in front of her bedroom window. At virtually the same instant, just a few houses down Petőfi út, Feri, confined to his bed with a bad cold and a case of Kaiser *sör*, awoke in an inebriated haze to find a new pair of *gumicsizma*—made by the very best company in Győr—beside his front door.

Further up in the vineyard that morning, Roland entered his parents' winemaking house on Szent Györgyhegy to find, to his amazement and delight—nestled right between the wooden casks that held his family's precious Olaszrizling and Balaton Chardonnay—his missing wooden hand. And Kormány Lajos, when he went out to feed the horses that day, was greeted by the ravenous *baahhhing* of two young black baby sheep.

That night, all was well in the small village of Hegymagas once more. Fischer and the Mayor, in a rare spirit of mutual affection and camaraderie, lifted a glass in Etus's honor at the *Italbolt,* joined by Roland, cradling his glass in his prosthetic arm. Feri, meanwhile—cold, hangover and all—was walking up and down Széchenyi út, proudly displaying his new rubber boots and humming a Hungarian version of "Love Me Tender."

Even Kormány Lajos, in a rare spirit of conviviality and peace, could be found at yet another table in front of the pub, playing chess with—of all people—Árpi. But best—and, many people felt, most potent—of all in restoring the village's usual atmosphere of tranquility and mutual affection was the scent of Etus's fish soup, simmering in a gigantic kettle in front of the post office, wafting its way all the way up to Árpi's vineyard and the appreciative nostrils of the new dog, Attila József, that Kormány had bought for her. The soup smelled—Kormány Lajos himself would later admit—as good, perhaps, as his own mother's had once, and its aroma, he also acknowledged, was far more likely to prevail.

THE GREATEST JEWISH-AMERICAN LOVER
IN HUNGARIAN HISTORY

At the ripe middle age of fifty-five, after some twenty-five years of skimming along the surface of various occupations and academic and literary pursuits without every having developed a firm commitment to his work, Marcus Bergmann finally decided to what it was he wanted to devote the rest of his life.

Like Hermione in D.H. Lawrence's *Women in Love,* he no longer believed in his own universals—they were a sham. He no longer believed in his own inner life—it was a trick. He no longer believed in the spiritual world—it was an affectation. Unlike his moral and literary betters, he was a man not very happy without the residues of some rectal or cunnilingual passion on his face. Nor had he committed, he felt, enough moral transgressions he felt truly ashamed of, and he was resolved, now in middle-age, to use what time he had left to rectify his ways. In the final resort, it was Mammon, the flesh, and the devil in whom he believed, and he longed, like so many men, for the mutually exclusive pleasures of being calmed by marriage and excited by romance.

"I would like to be the greatest Jewish-American Lover

in Hungarian history," he remarked to his neighbor, the eminent Hungarian writer Kepes, as they walked one evening among the vineyards of Szentgyörgyhegy. "I would like to be more successful a lover of Hungarian women than Endré Ady or Füst Milán or Gyula Illyés or Attila József . . . I would like to be more successful, even, than *you*."

Kepes, to be sure, had had no small reputation as a lover in his youth, numbering among his paramours, in addition to myriad young Hungarian beauties, married and unmarried, and the leading prostitutes in Budapest's many tawdry and elegant brothels, such international celebrities as Gloria Steinem, Wislawa Szymborska, Oriana Fallaci, and—the proudest of all his conquests—Susan Sontag. But now, slowed down a bit as he approached his seventieth year, distracted by the erotic demands of his significantly younger third wife, and somewhat dazed by the aftereffects of Hungarian palinka and Moroccan marijuana, the aging satyr seemed willing to hand over his mantel to a relatively younger aspirant such as Bergmann, and Bergmann seemed hardly opposed to taking on the challenge.

Bergmann, of course, had undergone an apprenticeship of his own in matters sybaritic during his four years of living and teaching in Budapest, where he had not infrequently availed himself of the myriad escort services and conveniently located "night clubs" adjacent to his writing studio—not to mention of his seductively beautiful, thong-embellished, willing female students. One of the latter had even been so kind as to inform him that American students who pressed charges of date rape and/ or sexual harassment against acquaintances and professors were known by their Hungarian counterparts as "virgin prostitutes," a term which, they felt, captured American women's strangely oxymoronic cohabitation of flirtatiousness with Puritanism.

Now, however, Bergmann had graduated to bigger, better— and, alas, significantly rarer—conquests, one failed and recidivistic attempt among them having been the Mayor, Horvath's, nineteen-year-old daughter, who had been deflowered just the summer before by Kepes's enviably youthful and available son, Benze. Having successfully wrestled her to the ground of the Horvaths' well-secluded, grass-covered backyard the summer before when everyone in her family was away (Bergmann's policy vis à vis seduction was the exactly opposite of the recently announced date rape guidelines in the U.S., namely *pounce first, ask later*), Bergmann had sufficiently aroused the young future lawyer with gentle blowings in the ear and kisses to the neck to have her ask, breathlessly, whether he was in possession of a condom. His negative answer, however, sadly terminated the afternoon's activities and left young Anikó's registry of lovers standing at the lonely integer of a single, radically inexperienced, Kepes.

Since Bergmann's wife and young son were now in the habit of making their annual Hegymagas appearance only in early August, Bergmann found himself with at least a month or two in early summer in which his amorous pursuits might both branch out and blossom forth. Attempting to take full advantage of this annual hiatus in his conjugal life, the latest target of his amorous aspirations was one Flavia Kunze, a conspicuously endowed, ravenously beautiful, and seductively dressed polyglot bartender at a nightclub called COLORS in nearby Kesthély, whom Bergmann had happened (and hoped, yet, to jump) on when he had stopped to ask directions to a nearby garden center the week before.

Flavia spoke perfect French, being the product of a French mother and Magyar father, and, from what Bergmann could tell, had been blessed with the finer attributes of both cultures: breathtakingly beautiful Hungarian cheekbones, charmingly alluring French eyes, and a body so curvaceous its contours might have been arranged at a summit meeting between the Danube Bend and the Loire River Valley.

"You are very direct," Flavia suggested to Bergmann when, hardly five minutes after making her acquaintance, he invited her to stop by his house in Hegymagas for a "late nightcap" after she got off from work. "Yes," Bergmann concurred, "I'm not someone who believes in wasting time."

"But I'm engaged," Flavia replied, her eyes suggesting that the enterprise was, nonetheless, not without hope.

"And I am married," Bergmann rejoindered. "And life is short."

Life, indeed, was short, and when, later that night, the ravishing eyes of Flavia Kunze looked down on Bergmann by candlelight as she straddled him into what seemed to him the closest proximity to human happiness one could know, Bergmann thanked whatever gods there were, not for his unconquerable soul, but, rather, for the persistence of his lusts, and for their occasional satisfaction.

"Oh, oh, oh, oh," moaned Flavia as her penetrating French pupils gazed down at penetrating Bergmann. "I am riding you and bouncing up and down."

"Oh, oh, oh," countered Bergmann in that universal rhapsodic speech that knew neither accents nor borders. "You are riding me and bouncing up and down, and," he elaborated, perfectly mimicking a French accent, "eet ees very very good."

Bergmann was, he realized, a lucky man: he was in Hungary—home to some eighty percent of the world's porn actresses, and the production center of a nearly equal percentage of its porn movies—a country in which the bedroom, blessedly, was still a safe distance from the penumbral adumbrations of political correctness and ideology. His good luck had simply been the confluence of two propinquitous events: The Hungarians loved to fuck. He loved to fuck as well. *Bingo!*

But, Bergmann also knew that, at fifty-five, one's hours of tumescence and concupiscence were fast running out: what loomed ahead were Viagra, Prozac, perhaps even the erectile pump. So there was no time to waste. No time to waste, and no wasting time. Bergmann was a man with a mission, a projectile with a target, an angel without mercy, a free-floating middle-aged libido eager to land almost anywhere.

"*Sexy vagy,*" Zsuzsa Kovacs, the notoriously widowed femme fatale of nearby Kovagöors, whispered in his ear one night as he made his way past the bar of her popular restaurant toward the men's room. *"Es te, sexy vagy,"* Bergmann returned the compliment, taking advantage of the dialogue's directness to fondle her left buttock. It was only a few hours later that, with Zsuzsa's lover of the moment, the piano player, still playing "Gloomy Sunday" (*Szomorü Vasarnap*) on the piano downstairs, Bergmann found himself not at all gloomily entwined in Zsuzsa Kovacs' ample flesh. It was a fine country, this Hungary, he had to admit . . . a fine place for a hungry man.

For Bergmann's wife, of course, Bergmann's amatory escapades—difficult to disguise upon her annual arrival, when numbers of lovely and sparsely clad Hungarian women came over to greet her husband at various Balaton beaches and restaurants— were not exactly a source of comfort. Though well schooled in the old European custom of casting one's eyes the other way, the other way, in Bergmann's case, seemed little more than an avenue from which the growing plethora of her husband's amorous conquests would enter the scene, nor did the occasional black or bright red thong that Bergmann had somehow, perhaps Freudianly, failed to remove from his underwear drawer do much to alleviate her burgeoning fantasies. Her husband, there was no denying it, was a womanizer, plain and simple, and whether the objects of his amorous ambitions submitted willingly or not was of little real comfort.

Kepes, meanwhile, fresh from having delivered a lecture entitled "On Seduction" at a conference on the same subject in Hamburg, observed the sentimental exploits of his American neighbor with no small amount of amusement and compassion. "Seduction's hero," Kepes had informed his none-too-abstractly interested audience, "is a mysterious figure who steps forward out of the unknown, who we cannot explain, who sees through us, but whom we cannot see through." Kepes knew all too well both the pleasures and the problems following one's more lustful impulses could lead to, and, having recently acknowledged that his own career among the minefields and mattresses of amorous desire was drawing to a close, he nonetheless, found it both entertaining and enticing to bear witness to someone's else's.

"He is headed for trouble, our friend Bergmann," he observed to his wife Julia, "but he will at least have a great deal of fun along the way."

Bergmann, indeed, was having a lot of fun along the way. He was no Wilt Chamberlain, to be sure, but the numbers, nonetheless, were adding up: Kunzes, Horvaths, Jovanoviches, Kovacses, all those lovely *c*s and *z*s. The world, if not his oyster, was surely potentially his *palacsinta*, if he just played his cards right. And if the great Hungarian whore, Ciccolina, could run for parliament, and *win,* in Italy, why couldn't Bergmann—merely a humble American writer from New York—at least become the greatest Jewish-American lover in Hungarian history? He had, after all, been born on what was to become International Women's Day, an occasion he now saw no reason not to think of as a perpetual celebration of his being born, and re-born, into the arms, and between the thighs, of the united women of the world.

Rhapsodically, while his wife remained in France, Bergmann cruised the beaches and brothels of the Balaton: *Szigliget, Badacsony, Abrahamhegy, Refülop, Kesthély, Balatongyörök,* singing a parody of a recently highly popular pop song that was constantly being played on Danubius radio:

> *A little bit of Monika in the sun*
> *A little bit of Zsuzsa on the run*
> *A little bit of Csilla on my face*
> *A little bit of Nóra everyplace . . .*

and so on. The names read like menu items from some heavenly restaurant, some erotic smorgasbord at an all-you-can-eat casino in Las Vegas, where the prices were low and the possibilities unlimited.

"The problem with you," Bergmann's lovely wife, Beatrice, intoned, like Judith incarcerated in Bluebeard's castle, "is that you want all the benefits of married life without any of the obligations. You are simply a child in a man's clothing."

"I have nothing at all against married life," Bergmann would reply. "It's merely married *sex* I'm not all that wild about.

"Even animals," he added, as though to drive home his point, "rarely mate in captivity."

Yet, he often had to admit to himself, his wife's accusations embodied a certain truth: He *was* a fifty-five-year-old child, dressed—though only occasionally—like a man. "From his own point of view," Kepes had told his Zurich audience, "the seducer is an immature personality, a psychopath who has not yet grown into his children's shoes, who has learned nothing from his experiences, who fails to think of what will come next, of what he will do with his acquisitions."

Still, Bergmann was learning something from his experiences: he was learning of the great variety, and diversity, of satisfactions that could be acquired through the nose and mouth. He was learning that no two women—and, more importantly, the *love* of no two women—were ever alike. He was learning that pleasure was life's only true justice, to leave morality and decency to the preachers and would-be saviors.

And as for his son's shoes?—What of them? Bergmann gazed down at the pair on the floor beside him—a mere size thirty-eight . . . still six sizes smaller than his own.

There's still plenty of time to grow into those, he thought to himself. *Still plenty of time to die back down to a young boy's size.*

THE WHORES

"Prostitution especially is a matter in which it makes all the difference whether you see it from above or from below."
—Robert Musil, *The Man Without Qualities*

The whores, who had been situating themselves for years along the more touristic highway between Balatonfüred and Kesthély, had recently expanded their workplace. To Bergmann's shock and amazement, they were now brazenly stationed, some five-hundred meters apart, along the otherwise tree-overhung and tranquil rural road leading from the county seat of Tapolca to the artist colony of Szigliget some eight kilometers away.

Dropped off at their work places by their local pimps— rather hefty, gold-chained Hungarians from Transylvania driving imported German cars—they stationed themselves along the roadside in their various transparent and flesh-clinging garments, smoking and listening to music on their Russian-made Walkmans, and creating a sequence of mini bottlenecks along the rural road, as male commuters between the two towns negotiated for various services and times.

On at least one occasion, the novelist Kepes's own son, Kristof, had scarcely avoided a head-on collision with one—a thin, colicky Gypsy girl dressed in bright red as she emerged from an assignation in the nearby woods, and Kepes himself had, on occasion, found the beckoning fingers and hips of their various offerings a kind of allure as he made his way between his favorite drinking venues—*kocsmas* and *sörözös*—in the two villages.

Whores, of course, were a way of life in Central Europe, professionals as honorable or dishonorable as any other, but it was, somehow, this having the trade plied so much "in the face" of the local children and their widowed grandmothers that at first upset Bergmann, and especially his wife Beatrice, and led him to think that—his youthful and not-so-youthful detours into a harlot's lap notwithstanding—this might be a matter to be taken up directly at the next meeting of the Hegymagas village council.

The village's mayor, Horváth, Bergmann knew, was a man with a weakness of his own for purchased flesh, and Bergmann couldn't quite imagine that this latest manifestation of the new market economy was all that alarming to him. (He was quite sure, for that matter, he had glimpsed Horváth's own rusted green Lada parked suspiciously at the side of a ditch along the road one early evening.)

For Bergmann and his son, on the other hand, the whores also provided a welcome bit of entertainment along the road leading from their summer home to Lake Balaton. On one such outing, Bergmann had affectionately nicknamed the regulars in honor of his favorite Hungarian dishes: *töltött káposzta* (Stuffed Cabbage) for the girl who usually wore a pale mini-skirt without underwear, and who waved enthusiastically whenever Bergmann drove by; *rántott csirkemell* (Fried Chicken Breast) for the most Gypsy-looking of the group, a deeply dark-skinned girl decked in a wide variety of earrings and bracelets, but little else; *somlói galuska* (Chocolate Bread Pudding) for the rather husky one invariably clad in tight, white pants and a black blouse, unbuttoned to the waist, and *hideg gyümölcsleves* (Cold Fruit Soup) for the girl who, for some reason, always turned away when Bergmann drove by, revealing only her indelicately exposed backside.

From Bergmann's point of view, at least, the *crème de la crème* among the offerings was Chocolate Bread Pudding, not so much for the clearly visible thin filament of thong—a long-time favorite of his among allurements—her tight white pants revealed, but, rather, for her knowing smile and milky, Slavic cheeks and high cheekbones, which set her apart from her rather dark, somewhat downcast, sisters.

On one occasion—not quite certain whether she was relieving herself, or merely servicing a client—Bergmann had even observed Chocolate Bread Pudding stooped, bare-bottomed, in the adjacent field, a position which had not kept her from sending a smile and a wave of her hand his way, and which only served to increase Bergmann's admiration, both for her friendliness and, it seemed, her versatility.

Horváth the mayor, on the other hand, being hardly a connoisseur of subtlety—judging, at least, from the usually location of his car—preferred Stuffed Cabbage, a choice Bergmann could easily relate to, but which somehow seemed, as Bergmann's wife might have put it, too *"ordinaire"* even for Bergmann's rather proletarian tastes.

At any rate, judging from the fact that they took up their positions promptly at sunrise seven days a week, and refused to vacate them until well after sunset, business seemed to be booming for the girls. The Tapolca-Szigliget road—which Bergmann had once dubbed "the road less traveled"—also seemed to benefit from the increase in visual enticements that now lined its shoulders, as more and more spiffily polished BMWs and Mercedeses, proudly bearing the D's and A's of their beloved Deutschlands and Austrias, took to navigating its narrow-shouldered curves.

"What are they selling?" Bergmann's son Isaac, approaching his twelfth birthday, inquired one day as they drove past the breast-and-buttock display along the Hungarian roadside.

"Themselves," Bergmann, a master of the literal, replied. "They are selling themselves."

"Oh," his son rejoined. "That's very interesting, Papa."

It *was*, indeed, interesting, Bergmann supposed, and, much as the presence of the whores along this formerly bucolic country road had upset him at first, he was slowly growing accustomed to their presence, and coming to consider them part of the local landscape and color.

"Welcome to Hegymagas," he remarked jokingly to Kepes one afternoon, as the two of them drove past desperately beckoning Stuffed Cabbage on their way from the Lake, "center, along with Bangkok and Havana, of the world's sex tourism industry."

"Yes," Kepes concurred, apparently not all *that* humored by Bergmann's numbering his native village among the centers of the world's sex trade, "it *is* quite amazing, to have these girls standing here, in the very place where my grandmother once sold cabbage and corn. In my day, at least," he continued nostalgically, "the whores had the decency to keep to the Night Clubs, where you at least didn't have to buy them right in front of your friends and neighbors."

Bergmann, in fact, confident that no one he knew would be passing by, *had* stopped at Chocolate Bread Pudding's station one night on his way back from a sunset swim to inquire as to the cost of her various services.

"Mennibe kerül?" he had asked in imperfect Hungarian as Chocolate Bread Pudding, dangling her headphones from one wrist and taking a deep drag of a long, skinny cigarette, walked over to his car, black thong underwear beckoning, *à la* Monica Lewinsky, from beneath her slacks.

"Sprechen Sie Deutsch?" she immediately replied, staring at the Berlin license plates on Bergmann's VW Golf. (Bergmann had purchased the car during a Fulbright year in Berlin.)

"Ja, ein bisschen," Bergmann, embarrassed by his failure to be convincing in Hungarian, replied, *"de nagyon szeretek beszélni magyarul."* Bergmann *liked* speaking Hungarian, far more than he liked speaking his own, historically tainted, mother tongue.

Chocolate Bread Pudding smiled her highly likeable Russian smile. "For you," she said in Hungarian, stroking Bergmann gently on the arm and motioning to the field, "just three-thousand forints an hour."

Bergmann was impressed, not to mention flattered. For that amount, in Budapest, you could hardly get a Big Mac. In the States, you had to travel to rural Louisiana to find a whore at that price—and God only knew what else you might get in the bargain.

Chocolate Bread Pudding motioned, first toward the field again, then to Bergmann's car. "Your choice," she said, this time in German. "Whatever is the most comfortable for you . . . *Oder vielleicht,"* she suddenly added, as if by way of an afterthought, *"haben Sie ein Haus?"*

The thought of bringing Chocolate Bread Pudding back to Hegymagas and entertaining her in his house, formerly the domicile of the village priest, half humored and half repulsed Bergmann, who countered with a lie: *"Nein, ich habe leider kein Haus."*

Just as Bergmann spoke, none other than Horváth emerged from the field across the road, followed closely by Stuffed Cabbage, still fastening her skirt. At the sight of Bergmann negotiating for similar services right before his eyes, the Mayor's face broke out, first into an enormous blush, then into a smile.

"Jó napot kivánok, szomszéd," he called out, waving lightheartedly. "Good afternoon, neighbor . . . *Hogy van?"*

"Just fine," Bergmann, flustered at first, but then quickly regaining his composure, waved back. *Ah, men,* he thought, *one of a kind at heart . . .* or, rather, below the heart.

Despite the obvious camaraderie in their situation, Bergmann found the Mayor's presence a kind of soporific to his excitement. Patting Chocolate Bread Pudding affectionately on the ass, he muttered a muted "maybe later" in Hungarian, and headed back toward the lake.

***

Now, however, it was summer's end, St. Stephen's Day, festival of Hungary's patron saint, and peregrinations of the vacation period, about to arrive. Bergmann was beginning to feel a wave of nostalgia *vis à vis* the aggregated women of the day who had lent such color and—with the exception of Cold Fruit Soup, just now seeming to warm to his presence—conviviality to his daily meanderings.

Why not, he suggested to Kepes and the Mayor one slightly inebriated evening when the three of them were sharing a table at the village *kocsma,* have a small good-bye "party" for the girls, who, after all, had proven a rather innocuous, and even entertaining, addition to the summer sights?

Horváth, who was to be up for re-election that fall, hesitated, as did Kepes, who seemed to recall his earlier, rather moralistic, pronouncements . . . and his grandmother. Yet, after an additional *pálinka* or two, the idea seemed to take on a certain appeal to all involved—what with the Mayor's wife off visiting relatives in Debrecen, and most of the other wives and children having already returned to Budapest to prepare for the school year.

Finally, with a rousing *egészségetekre* ("to your health") and a click of glasses, the deal was made: Bergmann, who seemed to have the most cordial relations with the group, was charged with inviting the girls to a *buli* at the Mayor's house on the night of the 20th, just as the fireworks would be going off along the Lake.

***

Fried Chicken Breast, wearing a bright yellow blouse that only served to accent her dark, olive skin, and her usual display of bracelets and earrings, arrived first, accompanied by a burly Transylvanian in a bright turquoise shirt, who also sported a thick gold chain around his neck and a watch whose face was almost the size of a wall clock. Bergmann, who thought the girls, for some reason, would arrive alone, tried hard to disguise his disappointment as the twosome entered the Mayor's house, already reeking of *pálinka.*

"*Jó estet kivánok,*" Fried Chicken Breast's date announced in a booming voice. "*Guten Abend.*"

"Guten Abend," replied Bergmann, giving in to the fact that German would be the evening's common vernacular. *"Ich bin froh dass Ihr hier seid."*

Within ten minutes, Stuffed Cabbage and Cold Fish Soup—each wearing a short black dress and brazenly exposed white thong—arrived, followed by Chocolate Bread Pudding, decked entirely in transparent white, and another woman, dressed in a bright green body suit, who was introduced merely as a "friend." Bergmann thought he recognized her from an outpost just over the tracks in Tapolca.

All the girls seemed already intimate with Chocolate Bread Pudding's date, who greeted each one with a lingering kiss and a familiar pinch on the (rear) cheek. Following his initial surprise, Bergmann couldn't help observing, to his satisfaction and relief, that—with the unexpected addition of Chocolate Bread Pudding's friend—there was now an appealing imbalance of five women and only four men.

From a corner of the living room, the voice of Koncz Zsuzsa, the Hungarian analog to Judy Collins, was singing songs of unrequited love and failed romance, and—before he knew what was happening to him—Cold Fruit Soup, of all people, had taken Bergmann by the arm, and was leading him, cheek to cheek, around the living room floor, her right thigh planted seductively between his legs. The Mayor, much to his delight, was likewise occupied with Stuffed Cabbage, and even Kepes, never much of a dancer, was leading Fried Chicken Breast in awkwardly unsyncopated rhumba-like steps around the living room.

Only Chocolate Bread Pudding and her friend in the green body suit, seated on the Mayor's sofa with the Transylvanian, smoking something that didn't quite resemble a cigarette, had not yet joined in the merriment. She waved gaily to Bergmann from the sofa, smiling her usual seductive smile and mouthing the words *"nächsten Tanz"* while massaging the Transylvanian's large, muscular thigh. The girl in green, meanwhile, was imbibing large beakerfuls of pálinka and singing a melancholy song in what Bergmann believed to be Rumanian. She winked at Bergmann, tactfully daubing a small drop of pálinka on each of her well-exposed breasts.

Suddenly, and quite unexpectedly, the front door of the Mayor's house flew open and there, back early from her sister's house in Debrecen, stood Hizzoner's wife, Dóra *néni*, holding a large tureen of her cousin's fish soup in both hands.

"Édesem!" The Mayor, unceremoniously releasing Stuffed Cabbage from his embrace, addressed his rather bewildered-looking wife with that tenderest of Hungarian terms, "What in the world are *you* doing here?"

Quickly regaining her composure and straightening her pale blue peasant dress as she placed the tureen on the kitchen table beside the Transylvanian's pálinka, the Mayor's wife turned to the assembled revelers, a smile forming at the corner of her mouth. Then, looking more or less like the typical Hungarian wife addressing a group of invited guests, she cheerfully asked, "Would anyone like some soup?"

Speechlessly, the gathered women of the highway and men of the village rose to make their way toward the soup. As they did, Dóra Horváth took her husband's freshly-liberated hand, kicked her shoes off in the direction of the sofa, and said: "Now, *édesem,* let's dance!"

Bergmann watched the Mayor and his wife break into a kind of celebrative Hungarian polka and sat himself down on a large stuffed chair. A profound feeling of well-being suddenly came over him. It had been a long, mostly satisfying summer—

highlighted by a total solar eclipse one hundred percent visible along the Balaton, long evenings of Olaszrizling and Chardonnay in Kepes's backyard, and morning hikes along the relatively tame, once-volcanic hills that punctuated the Balaton wine country.

Life, he thought to himself, as Chocolate Bread Pudding rose from the sofa—her thong rising in its nest of flesh to accompany her—and headed in his direction, *life was good after all.*

Koncz Zsuzsa was singing another brokenhearted song on the Mayor's antiquated stereo; Kepes and Fried Chicken Breast rumbaed by, reeking of fermented plums; the Mayor, with his wife now on one arm and Stuffed Cabbage on the other, was heading for the sofa. Outside, on the two solitary streets of the village of Hegymagas, the air rife with the smell of chickens and ripening grapes, the crescent moon was at a slant.

Bergmann took a deep breath, enthusiastically encircling Chocolate Bread Pudding with his arms. All was well with the world, he thought, and would likely continue to be . . . at least for the rest of that sultry August night. He would wake the next day, merely to welcome back his ordinary life—where only a stray chicken would be standing, any longer, alongside the Szigliget road, and Chocolate Bread Pudding's black blouse would be hanging in a closet somewhere, buttoned all the way up.

***

Bergmann was forced to acknowledge when he arrived the following June that the previous summer must not have been as successful a season as he had thought for his newfound roadside friends.

Filled with anticipation as he drove toward Szigliget the morning of his arrival, he saw, to his dismay, that, of the previous summer's not unappealing quartet, only Cold Fruit Soup—still offering only her backside as Bergmann passed, but dressed, now, is opaque blue pants and a rumpled white blouse—remained at her station, accompanied along the country road not by three, but merely two, of her fellow workers.

The second girl—a hefty, tousle-haired creature with a grim-faced expression, wore tight black shorts, running shoes without socks and a maroon T-shirt through which one could get more than a hint of bulbous, prematurely drooping breasts. Bergmann immediately nicknamed her *Túró Gombóc* (Cheese Dumpling), in honor of the rotund and somewhat sweet-sour image she projected.

How incredibly unabating, thought Bergmann as he drove past Cheese Dumpling—her platinum-dyed hair shimmering in the Balaton light, her visage ablaze with a bored prurience—the male lust for fornication! How remorselessly undifferentiated it could be, at times, in its choice of objects! And filled with such despair.

It occurred to him, gazing disconsolately at Cheese Dumpling's dark skin and thick ankle bracelets, that she and Chicken Breast might even be sisters. Nonetheless, she evoked only a pale glimmer of her co-workers' more luminous presences of the summer before, and it seemed—at least, from the sight of her picnicking alone most afternoons beneath a shadowing chestnut—that the other commuters between Tapolca and Szigliget felt likewise.

Just down the road from the shade-strewn outpost the two girls now occupied, stood—wearing a slightly grease-stained, chocolate brown halter top, tight blue Day-Glo bicycling shorts and white go-go boots—the final vector of this year's Unholy Trinity, a solarium-fried and irredeemably unattractive lass whom Bergmann, in the company of his now twelve-year-old son, dubbed *Bableves* (Bean Soup) and who, to Bergmann's ever-categorizing mind, took the cake—or, rather, the soup—as the most unattractive specimen of the female gender yet placed in glaring contradistinction to the magnificent roadside plane trees and sunflowers.

"It sure seems like *Túró Gombóc* is a lot more popular than *Bableves,*" Isaac observed as they drove past ever-imploring Bean Soup, chugging on her bottle of *ásványvíz* (mineral water) and plugged into her Walkman like an out-of-work airline stewardess. "She's always standing there alone, while Túró Gombóc"—who was, indeed, a quetzal by comparison—"must be getting all the business."

As for Stuffed Cabbage and Chocolate Bread Pudding, Bergmann could now locate only a bevy of Hungarian crows and a solitary turkey vulture at what once had been their outposts. Horváth, too, seemed more than a bit depressed by the personnel changes that had taken place from the previous year. That very afternoon—on his way home after consoling himself at a local *söröző* in Szigliget—Bergmann spotted the Mayor's newly acquired 1974 Trabant parked along the side of the road, and Hizzoner engaged in what seemed a prolonged, and deeply troubled, conversation with Bean Soup. Their tête-à-tête unexpectedly terminated with the Mayor shaking a finger at the poor, newly conscripted girl, then leaving a patch of East German rubber along the roadside as he sped off in a huff.

Ah, the hardships of the new capitalist economy! thought Bergmann. *Its cruelties and unfeeling marketplace!* Yet, as he crisscrossed the countryside around the Balaton in the course of his daily rounds, Bergmann couldn't help but observe that, though the womanpower had diminished along the Tapolca-Szigliget road, there had been a corresponding increase in the number of girls now working the small side roads between Keszthely and Balatonszentgyörgy, and between Fenyód and Ordacsehi. The Transylvanians, Bergmann surmised, must, like all good socialists-turned-entrepreneurs, have re-assessed the situation, and decided there was better business to be done by redistributing their workers in smaller numbers over a broader range, subscribing to the mantra of the real estate industry: *location, location, location.*

The following week, however, an even more disturbing development took place. Bergmann returned from swimming at Szigliget beach to find a bright yellow warning sticker affixed to his rented car, parked in its usual spot along the dirt road just south of the paying lot. A bright red Hungarian steel boot was affixed to the passenger side front tire.

"Négy ezer forintot kérek," a hardly pubescent Hungarian police officer, followed closely by his companion, an equally young, pale-faced *bootmester*, greeted him affably. "That will be four thousand forints, please."

Bergmann reached into his pocket and rummaged about, coming up with the mere two two-hundred-forint notes he had with him.

"Kein Problem," the bilingual young officer smiling, offering to accompany him to whatever hidden resources lurked back home, *"wir können mit Ihnen nach Hause gehen."* And so, politely waving to Cheese Dumpling along the way, the two officers, closely taxiing behind Bergmann's rental Fiat, accompanied him to Hegymagas. There, upon payment of the four-thousand-forint ransom fee, along with an addition one-thousand forints for the parking violation, Bergmann was once

again released into his own custody and his lingering daydreams of the Girls of Summer.

The next morning, things went from bad to worse, as—doing a robust fifty-five kilometers per hour in a thirty kilometer zone as he crossed the tracks leading from Tapolca toward Raposka—Bergmann was greeted by the waving flashlight of yet another Hungarian civil servant, this one a young, attractive female police officer, who politely waved him over to the side of the road and began mercilessly scolding him in her native tongue.

"Beszélek csak egy kicit magyarul," Bergmann pleaded in nearly perfect pidgin Hungarian, whereupon the young officer, now leaning against her police vehicle along with two male officers and another young woman, politely informed him in German that he would have to personally go to the Hegymagas post office the next morning and pay a ten-thousand forint fine. Bergmann signed on the dotted line beneath the paragraph informing him, in several languages, that he was subject to being denied entry into Hungary in the future, should he fail to pay the fine or incur any further violations.

Deeply impressed—and very nearly impoverished—by what he experienced as the sudden spirit of law-abidingness that had erupted in this goulash-ridden former Communist backwater, Bergmann—with his by-now-well-practiced *"nagyon szépen köszönöm"* ("thank you very much")—got back into his car, fastened the seat belt, turned on the requisite front lights, and, maintaining a less-than-breathtaking fifty kilometers per hour, made his way home.

Nor was that the end of what was apparently that summer's onslaught of high-minded lawfulness. Bergmann was stopped twice more for speeding before St. Stephen's Day, and had his car booted a total of five times, including once at the Tapolca flea market, where he had never seen so much as a parking ticket handed out before. The very next day, what's more, Bergmann perambulated his way down the Szigliget road to the glaring absence—not merely of Stuffed Cabbage, Fried Chicken Breast and Chocolate Bread Pudding—but of Cold Fruit Soup, Cheese Dumpling and Bean Soup as well.

"What happened to Cheese Dumpling and Bean Soup?" Isaac, who harbored a fondness, both for girls *and* their namesake Hungarian dishes, asked as they drove past.

"I don't know," Bergmann, risking a joke he assumed was well beyond his son's still pre-adolescent appreciation, replied. "Maybe one of their customers ate them."

***

Devoured or not, only one girl—a dour-faced, rather tepid-looking ectomorph with dark oily skin always dressed in purple whom Bergmann dubbed *Magányos néni*—Aunt Lonely Hearts—would return for what remained of that summer. The poor creature, apparently not in demand by the various tipsy Hungarians and Austrian tourists who whizzed by without so much as a flickering brake light, spent most of her days seated dejectedly along the roadside sipping from her bottle of mineral water and mopping her brow with a yellow handkerchief.

Driving down the road one last time on his way to Budapest for his flight home, Bergmann passed just as Miss Lonely Hearts was being deposited along the roadside by two Transylvanians in a bright red BMW. As he drove by, offering his habitual, casual wave, their eyes suddenly met, and she, forlornly, waved back. There was, he suddenly noticed—as if coming, by surprise, upon a crucial moment of his own education—a deep sadness in her eyes. It was a purely human sadness, he realized, a sadness that had little, or nothing, to do with pudding or chicken breasts or cabbage—not even with cheese dumplings—and certainly not much to do with love.

MY FRENCH WIFE

"Why, Huck, doan' de French people talk de same way we does?"

"No, Jim, I couldn't understand a word they said—not a single word."

"Well, now, I be ding-busted! How dat come?"

"I don't know; but it's so. I got some of their jabber out of a book. Spose a man was to come to you and say Polly-voo-franzy—what would you think?

"I wouldn' think nuff'n; I'd take en bust him over de head. Dat is, if he warn't white. I wouldn't 'low no nigger to call me dat."

"Shucks, it ain't calling you anything. It's only saying do you know how to talk French."

"Well, den, why couldn't he say it?

"Why, he is a-saying it. That's a Frenchman's way of saying it."

—Mark Twain, *The Adventures of Huckleberry Finn*

"So, you have a French wife?" People invariably raise their brows when I mention mine. "Lucky you."

A French wife. A wife who is French, a girl from France. *Lucky you,* the world thinks. Having a French wife, most people suppose, is something special, something every man should aspire to. The French wife, like the Great Dane, like Irish Whiskey, like Belgian waffles, like Hungarian paprika, sends covetous chills through the world's great desirers, hard-ons straight into the groins of the world's exhausted satyrs.

And who, when one considers the great French wives of literature and history, can blame them? Marie Antoinette, supposedly a dynamo in the sack in addition to her generosity with cake, was a French wife, as were, in a manner of speaking, Georges Sand, Simone de Beauvoir, Colette, Anaïs Nin. Even Picasso's wife Jacqueline, we might remind ourselves, was once a French wife, as was the wife of the great French surrealist poet Aragon, whom he generously shared with most of his friends. And—while we're on the subject of being French, and of being a wife—who could possibly forget Charles Bovary's slightly peripatetic French wife, Emma?

The French wife evokes images of passionate nights, filled with *tendresse* as well, of lustful afternoons in light-filled Parisian *ateliers*, of *escargots au beurre* and *vin blanc* consumed in king-sized beds before the French wife, in an orgy of sexual bliss and olfactory aphrodisia, is consumed as well. Life with a French wife, the prevailing wisdom goes, is a perpetual bottle of *Châteuneuf du Pâpe* and a wheel of ripe brie, an endless feast of *paté de foie gras* and fresh chanterelles, creamy desserts always made *avec chocolat de Purycard*.

"So you have a French wife?" many a man mumbles in my ear, giving me the squeeze at parties and looking over my shoulder in search of my conjugal good fortune. "You lucky sonuvabitch."

Yes, I have a French wife. Made in France, just like *La Marseillaise*, like chèvre de Provence, like Brigitte Bardot and Jacqueline Bisset, French as Charles de Gaulle. 100% *produit de la France.* Yes, eat your hearts out, would-be cosmopolitans of the world. I have a French wife. And she is, indeed, French, little pointed nose and all.

But, gentle reader, lest you become carried away by your blind envy, your adulation of all that is foreign and other, it might be best to remember:

My wife, to be sure, is French. But she is also a wife.

One/*Un*

I met my French wife at an outdoor café on the Avenida de Amazonas in Quito, Ecuador, where I had stopped for a cup of coffee on my way to the Museum of Modern Art. It was a Sunday morning. I was, more or less, happy to be alone, a free bird, an enchilada in nobody's mouth but his own.

"Conozes la via hasta el museo?" I said in broken Spanish to the two young women sitting at the table next to me.

"Nous ne sommes pas Ecuadorenas, sommes françaises." The dark-haired, to-me-prettier one looked up. Her companion, my French wife-to-be, kept on shyly reading her mail. I've never much liked shy women . . . still don't. Or maybe I just like them better than I'm prepared to admit.

"Maybe you would like to spend the night with me, *non?*" my future French wife said to me that night while her dark-haired friend went to use the john at the fleabag hotel in Otavalo where the three of us were staying. She was wearing a yellow sweatshirt and bright purple pants, both of which made a nice contrast to her greying hair. She had, I couldn't avoid noticing during the bus ride, nice skin, a kind of melancholy beauty to her eyes.

Why not? I thought to myself. The French, I'd heard, were supposed to be great in bed, they didn't believe in too-frequent showers or armpit deodorants. A French woman had once lifted her arm to scratch her head in the seat next to me at a movie theatre in Avignon . . . and it was true. They could also cook to kill.

Why not? I figured. Why not?

***

"I don't really believe in Western medicine," my French wife-to-be said to me one night in Quito several days later. "Or in birth control pills."

"Well, what *do* you believe in then?" I asked naively.

"I take my temperature."

"And have you ever been pregnant?"

"Of course not. Have you?"

I'd been pregnant, in fact, five times—or, at least, responsible for the male half of that predicament—and wasn't all that eager for another visit to the abortion clinic, particularly in South America. But, fertile devil that I am, *"positivo para embarrasada"* said the small slip of paper left in the envelope bearing my French wife-to-be's name at the gynecological clinic in Quito several weeks later . . . *positive for pregnancy.*

"Well, so much for birth control," I said as we walked out of the clinic into the August Ecuadorian light.

"Eet's amazing," said my future French wife. "I don't understand it."

I felt like having some lunch, though a sad, uneasy feeling was beginning to gather in my stomach. For most of my forty years on the planet, I had been a free man. But now, something told me, I was on my way to having a French wife.

***

"It is almost impossible to find a good tomato in this country," said my French wife once we were back in Cambridge. "Almost everything you buy ees garbage."

My French wife was, I soon discovered, crazy about fruits and vegetables. In fact, *all* the French, I was soon to find out, are crazy about fruits and vegetables. "When I was picking fruits in the South of France," soon became, in fact, a kind of introductory clause to most of the French-accented sentences that reverberated through my household, inevitably leading to some final *dénouement* concerning "my friend Lucian's apricots."

My French wife's sister, Annick, I realized when she showed up that winter with her two hyperactive kids to visit us, also loved fruits. *"Les fruits ici sont vraiment horribles,"* she would say virtually every time she bit into a locally purchased peach or tomato, *"c'est un pays dégoutant."*

***

Silent as a stone at Cambridge dinner parties and literary events, on the subject of circumcision my French wife nonetheless had a great deal to say.

"I think eet is *barbaric*," she said when I first raised the subject, a term she was not reluctant to repeat to the Hillel rabbi, Ben Zion Gold, when he called to try and enlighten her on the differences between a *bris* and a hospital circumcision. "It is like sending your child to the butcher's."

"I wish that you will have a happy and healthy child," the Rabbi said, just before hanging up on her. "Millions of children have been circumcised all over the world," I offered, resorting to an evidentiary mode, "and they've all survived. . . . Some of them have even become Supreme Court justices and Nobel Prize winners."

"Yes," said my French wife. "And no one knows how traumatized or psychologically damaged they may have been by the experience. I will convert, I will move to Israel, I will learn Hebrew, I will do *anything*. . . . But I won't send my son to the butcher's for the sake of some barbaric and outdated religious ritual."

My wife's a Catholic, a country girl from the valley of the Luberon. Her grandmother on her father's side gave birth to sixteen children, her mother's mother to nine. And not a circumcised pecker in the bunch. "We don't do thees," my wife explains to me, "in France. Eet makes men afraid of pleasure."

When her two nephews, Marlon and Rudi, had come to stay with us that winter, I watched the long, skinny, untampered-with air-hoses of their penises bob up and down like young girls' ponytails as they slid and skittered around our house, playing with themselves like young boys tapping a tetherball.

"But my Don José works just fine," I would say, using the term we had adopted to refer to my organ when we first met in Ecuador, "and *I'm* circumcised."

"*Sometimes* eet works fine, Gringo," my French wife corrected me, smiling her mischievous, birdlike smile.

Having never ventured into even one of the Harvard libraries in the half year since her arrival in Cambridge, my French wife was now suddenly able to amass a rather remarkable database of anti-circumcision materials, filled with such unsubtly applied verbs as "crushed," "pinched," "sliced," "chopped," and "cleaved," and produced by such heretofore-unknown-to-me groups as the Anti-Circumcision League, Homeopaths Anonymous, Protect-Your-Child, etc.

THE BRUTAL RITE OF CIRCUMCISION blurted out one pamphlet filled with lurid photographs of bloodied members dressed in splints and surgical tape. **OUR SON'S CIRCUMCISION NIGHTMARE** read two parents' bone-chilling account of their son's near-dismemberment and subsequent lifelong traumas at the hands of the local *moyl*.

"Maybe you should come with me and actually *see* a circumcision," I offered, "instead of sending away for all this anti-Semitic propaganda."

"I would faint," my French wife, a confirmed vegetarian, replied. "I don't need to see one . . . I *know* what it's like. And eet ees the kind of thing I wouldn't even do to a bull," she continued, "and I will *never* do eet to my baby, *Gringo*."

"It's just as I thought," I replied, sulkily.

"*What* ees as you thought?"

"The French," I said, sounding so much like my parents that it even terrified me. "They are all anti-Semites."

"I should have married a Jewish girl, like Donald did," I ventured to a friend at a colleague's newborn son's circumcision some weeks later.

"Don't be silly," my friend replied. "Just think . . . you have a French wife. You lucky dog."

***

"I feel," my French wife says, in what I initially believe to be a refreshingly candid acknowledgement of her grammatical difficulties with the English language, "like I have falling butts."

"You're not all that great with the 'ands' and 'ifs' and 'intos' either, if you want to know the truth," I reply.

"Since Isaac was born," she continues, ignoring my remark, "I feel like all my inner organs have been falling out." My wife, good French boarding school Catholic girl that she once was, is ever aware of the kinds of things that will arouse a man's erotic imagination. "I theenk I pushed too hard trying to get him out when he was born."

"It was *you* who wanted natural childbirth, as I remember it."

"Yes, but now I just don't feel the same as I once did. Maybe eet is also the bad fruits that you have here."

"Yes," I shrugged, "most likely it's the fruits."

***

"These Americans," says my French wife, "arc so disgustingly friendly. They ask you 'How are you?' when they really couldn't care less and are always telling you to 'Have a nice day' when they don't care what kind of day you have."

"They're just being friendly. It certainly beats the French way of treating you like a piece of shit just because you can't perfectly speak *la langue maternelle*."

"You're deviating the conversation again. I'm not talking about zee French, I'm talking about zee Americans." My French wife accuses me of "deviating the conversation" whenever my responses aren't precisely to her liking.

"And I'm talking about being friendly, rather than being hostile."

"Zee French aren't hostile . . . they are merely 'onest."

"Yup, honestly unfriendly . . . like you are." Superficial charm, to say the least, was not one of my French wife's leading attributes. ("All the personality of a mature garden hose," was how an old friend I lost when I married her put it.)

"Count your blessings," says my wife, echoing my father's familiar refrain, "you are lucky to have a French wife."

***

Cheating, according to my French wife, is another one of the attributes that differentiate the French from our typical, puritanical

Americans.

"When I was at chiropractic college," she once told me, "all zee French were always cheating and lending papers to each other—we were very proud of it—and the Americans acted as if we were committing some terrible crime . . . they just couldn't *believe* we would cheat so openly."

"Well," I looked up, "cheating doesn't tend to be one of those things Americans are terribly proud of . . . or, at least, they don't advertise."

"That's because zey are too busy advertising for everything else," countered my French wife.

Loans, apparently, were yet another matter my French wife didn't have many qualms about cheating on. She'd attended chiropractic school in California before we met in Ecuador, and once, in passing, mentioned some loans she had taken out during her four years there and never repaid.

"About how much was it?" I'd once asked, before, in a ceremony conducted by a Unitarian theology student friend and lasting all of eight minutes (our little progeny already kicking in my French wife's belly), we tied the knot.

"Oh, about fifteen thousand dollars, I theenk."

The sum—and the fact of the loan itself—had been immediately filed away in my slightly repressed unconscious with the thought that it was hardly a life-threatening amount . . . until, that is, the October evening when I found my wife (right after being informed that she had passed the licensing exam that would finally allow her to contribute to our sagging financial situation) sitting glumly on our bed, a funereal pallor blanketed firmly across her pointedly French features.

"What's the matter? Did somebody die?"

"I have something to tell you."

"You're not pregnant again, are you?"

"No. But do you remember those loans I took out during chiropractic school?"

"How could I forget? I guess you'll have to start paying those fifteen thousand bucks back now."

"Well, eet seems that zey are a leetle bit more than just feefteen zousand dollars." In moments of stress, my French wife's French accent tended to become even more pronounced.

"Like how much is a leetle?" I now tended, under stress, to develop a bit of a French accent myself.

"Here . . . look." My wife tossed me a terse telegram bearing the return address of the California Higher Education Assistance Corporation and the following cheerful message:

In re: Loan # 175038 BBL

Amount borrowed	*$44,674.23*
Accumulated interest	
(9/87- 10/92)	*$41,432.90*

PLEASE REMIT IMMEDIATELY $86,107.13

Dear Ms. Recamier:
It has come to our attention that the student loan referred to above, in the amounts indicated, remains unpaid and is highly delinquent. To avoid further legal action, please remit a check for the entire amount to the above address within the next ten days. Your prompt cooperation will avoid both legal action and serious possible consequences for your professional future.

> *Yours sincerely,*
> *Melvin P. Donner*
> *Director, California Higher*
> *Education Assistance Corp.*

"Eighty-six thousand bucks!" I felt my knees weaken, the blood rushing to my face. "Do you know how much fucking money that is?"

"They are crazy, zees Americans," says my French wife.

"*They're* crazy? What do you mean, *they're* crazy? You borrow forty-five thousand bucks, run out on them, don't tell the man you're about to marry that you've borrowed money up to your teeth, and then you say that *they're* crazy . . . Are you nuts?"

"In France we do not have to pay for zee universities at all."

"This isn't France. It's the United States of America."

"Eet's a crazy country, where you have to pay so many thousands of dollars just to get an education. I never thought I would ever be coming back here and have to pay off zees crazy loans."

"Well, in that case you should have thought of using something besides an oral thermometer for birth control."

"You are very funny. . . . Eet was *you*—don't you remember?—who couldn't get the condom on."

***

"Isn't it about time for us to get Isaac vaccinated?" I said to my French wife one morning when our son was about six months old.

"Vaccinated? Are you craaazy? I'm not going to have him vaccinated."

"You're not going to WHAT?" I stared at my son's uncircumcised penis, an organ which to my unworldly Jewish American eye increasingly resembled an aging piece of untrimmed corned beef.

"I'm not going to have him vaccinated. Children can die from zose vaccinations, don't you know?"

"I thought it was the *diseases* children died from. Ever heard of polio, tetanus, whooping cough, measles?"

"Eet's all propaganda from zeese American pharmaceutical companies. Eef you just allow a child to have these diseases, they develop their own immunities to zem and zey are much better off. All of you Americans are brainwashed by Western medicine and these rich drug companies."

"I never realized before that France bordered on Bangkok."

"Very funny. In France, *none* of my friends' children are vaccinated, and zey are all in perfect health."

"Listen, in this country you can't even get a kid into school without proof that he's been vaccinated."

"Eet's no problem. My sister will send us fake vaccination papers from France."

"Oh? Do you think she could provide us with some fake loan repayment papers as well?"

"Very funny, Gringo," says my French wife. "You are a very funny American."

"Are you crazy?" my friend John's wife Sally says to me several days later when she asks me where Isaac is having his pediatric exams. "You're not having your son vaccinated? If you ask me, you could be charged with negligent homicide for something like that. How are you going to feel if your son comes down with smallpox or polio or something like that?"

"They are all brainwashed," says my French wife.

"Yup," I shake my head, "according to you the whole United States is one big subcontinent of brainwashed zombies mutilating their kids with vaccines and circumcisions, and unable to grow a single decent piece of fruit."

"Except in California," says my French wife.

"Where you're probably on the Most Wanted List for loan fraud and tax evasion."

"Oh, Gringo," says my French wife, "you are a very funny man. A very, very funny man."

"Give the guy a break," John says to Sally. "He has a French wife, you know. The French are just a little bit different."

***

"Oh, *Gringo*," my French wife says to me, looking up from playing with our cat Chimborazo, "you are such a crazy man." She's called me *Gringo* since the day we met at that café in Quito, where she'd gone, she explained to me later, in the hope of meeting a dark-haired, olive-skinned Otavalo Indian.

It's Sunday. We've just made love for the first time in months, and are both feeling proud of ourselves, listening to Leonard Warren singing arias from *Il Forza del Destino* on the kitchen tape player.

I love my French wife—that is, insofar as I know what love is. Which means that some days I feel as though I couldn't live without her. Others, she's just a kind of weather—a dust storm, an inclemency. In large measure, I'm probably like most men . . . a grown boy who misses his mother. Part wildman, part homunculus, part trembling stick that just can't find a home. *"Je suis, bien sûr, un peu maternelle,"* my French wife says, and she is. She worries about my diet. She buys me vitamins.

"You and I are like flies," my friend Sonia, a linguist from Havana, says to me when I go over to her place to bitch about my marriage. "We buzz all over the place, making a lot of noise. But your wife," Sonia smiles with the pleasure of someone who has just incriminated themself from a safe distance, "she is an owl. She sits quietly up in the trees and observes. But, when she finally strikes—*whoosh!"*

All week, buzzing and hovering, landing and sighing, I've been contemplating Sonia's words. *"Tu es mon petit hibou,"* I coo at my French wife, a provincial girl from the Luberon.

"Eeet's *une chouette* in the feminine," my French wife corrects me. *"Et tu es mon moustique,"* she adds, smiling her pretty smile. Whenever I've loved a woman, whatever love may be, it's been a kind of craziness. But my French wife is calm, serene, collected . . . an owl high in the trees, waiting to strike.

"You need to learn to be a warrior," says a hyper-masculine friend of mine, a former captain in the Israeli army who became a Sikh. "You either have to learn to defend a woman to the death, or leave her and find someone else."

"But where's the war?" I keep asking.

"It's all a war," he says. *And who can argue with that?*

***

"You are, Gringo," my French wife likes to remind me, "a complicated man." And she's right: I *am* a complicated man. Love calls to me from the things of this world, and most of them are women.

In fact, women call out to me from almost everywhere—French women, Hungarian women, Asian women, Hispanic women . . . everything but American women, all of whom seem to me like bright green plaid, tasteless and ordinary. Some people say I have what the French call *une idée fixe*, that I'm what my friend Bob calls "a one-issue man," what Willa Cather, I think it was, called "that secondary social man, the lover." And it's true: if love is a single issue (which I doubt), then, yes, I'm a one-issue man.

But the truth of it is, I'm not ashamed. What great man, after all, *hasn't* been a one-issue man? Wasn't Martin Luther King a one-issue man? And what about Gandhi? The Marquis de Sade?

Elie Wiesel? Isn't Mother Theresa a one-issue man?

"It's not easy," I say in response to my wife's diagnosis of my complexity, "being a Great Man . . . or, for that matter, having a French wife."

"I know," she shakes her head compassionately, "and eet eesn't easy living with one either." My wife and I have agreed, tacitly and discreetly, to this Great Man Theory of my existence, much as it is contradicted by the actual realities. We both know, of course, that I am nervous, insecure, self-absorbed, prone to acute feelings of powerlessness, an occasional bed-wetter.

"It might just be a fact," Sonia, who hovers like a fly over my discontentments, informs me, "that, whenever you look your wife in the face, you see only your own emptiness." And she may, indeed, be right. For, deep down, my French wife and I both know what all men know: that women, for the most part, are stronger, securer, wiser, more resourceful than any man will ever be. The studies prove it. In fact, you don't even *need* the studies to prove it . . . just look any man in his sheepish, frightened face. Just read the panic-stricken libretto in their eyes when they are womanless.

Which is why the Great Man theory of my own being is so helpful to me in dealing with my French wife, *ma petite chouette*. It's a kind of psychological cross-dressing, giving me a kind of drag-queen entrée into the world of the well adjusted.

"You're a lucky woman, Frenchie," I reassure my wife from time to time, donning the glittered pantyhose of my battered psyche. "It's not every *vache qui rit* who gets to live with a Great Man."

"Oh, Gringo, I know," my French wife agrees, swaying the cat peacefully in her arms. "I am so lucky I can hardly believe eet."

***

The first time my French wife and I slept together, in the small Indian village of Otavalo just north of Quito, she asked me what I thought about infidelity. Like every man with his spidery psyche and forked tongue out to capture some prey, I told her I was all for it; that, just like Winston Churchill's views on democracy, it was the worst possible system . . . until, that is, you compared it with every other possible system.

Now that the walls have fallen in Berlin and Prague and Bucharest and Warsaw, I've begun to think of that night again, and of Winston Churchill. I also think a lot about Paul Newman's famous statement that he saw no reason to go out for hamburger when you had steak at home.

So now it's Sunday once again. We're at home, and I'm loving my French wife. At least, insofar as I know what love is. She looks great in the shifty April light. She is, I tell her, *"ma vache qui rit . . . ma petite chouette."*

"And you are *mon moustique fou,"* she says, kissing me on the cheek, then on the lips. "My crazy Gringo mosquito . . . even if you don't know what a good tomato is."

Our cat Chimborazo purrs. My son, his uncircumcised penis midway into the air, snores on his little bed. Leonard Warren, whom I watched drop dead on stage at the Met some thirty years ago, sings on from the kitchen. My French wife rubs my back in quick, circular motions, like a hovering fly. The world, some writer once said, is a wedding, not a circumcision.

Something tells me I am among the truly blessed.

Two/*Deux*

If, like me, you have a French wife, the chances, genetic and otherwise, are pretty good that you will also have an at least half-

French son, and—unless you're a terribly lucky man indeed—a French mother-in-law. *"Oh, mon chèr petit garçon,"* says my French mother-in-law Yvette during her weekly Sunday morning phone call, *"comme tu me manques!"* My French mother-in-law—in no small measure, I suspect, due to the fact that I am the only college-educated full-time wage-earner to ever marry into her family—has had an intense love affair with me from her daughter's very first letter, postmarked Quito, announcing that she had met *"l'homme de ma vie."*

"Quelle joie, d'avoir rencontré un homme comme ça," Yvette—whose own marriage was obviously more a product of revisionist fantasies than conjugal reality—perpetually consoled her daughter, whose own view of the matter, I'm sure, was beginning to differ, during a two-month visit to Cambridge early on in our marriage. A born-again widow who lives in a stone house without either electricity or plumbing—making her the only human being I know who, literally rather than metaphorically, buries her own shit—in a Benedictine community in Hâute Provence, Yvette proved not a much greater fan of our local produce than her two daughters, despite the glow of religiosity that suffused all her worldly relations.

"J'aime tout le monde, mais tout le monde me n'aime pas,"—I love all the world, but all the world doesn't love me—she offered as an explanation for her martyred condition. *"Et je t'aime vraiment et tendrement, mon beau fils,"* she would invariably add, expressing her more particularized affections. Never before had I—a Jewish boy from New York leading her betwixt and between the hundreds of churches of Boston and Cambridge—felt so loved by someone who hardly knew me. *"Tu*

avais vraiment de bonne chance d'avoir trouvé un mari comme ça," she perpetually repeated to her daughter, my French wife . . . *You are so lucky to have found a husband like that.*

***

"Je ne veux pas papa!" my son invariably cries out when I, the would-be circumciser, approach him in moments of crisis. "I DON'T WANT YOU." My son, like his mother, tends to be a homeopath where medical matters are concerned.

"J'aime les medicaments," he mumbles, bright-eyed, as my French wife pours a huge variety of homeopathic powders, supplements, vitamins, and other remedies down his four-year-old throat, making me feel, at least momentarily, sorry that the profession of pharmacist in France has traditionally been largely the domain of those possessing large amounts of inherited wealth.

"Papa," he says, prying open the refrigerator with the same delight his full-blooded American counterpart might feel entering a candy store. "Did you take your vitamins yet?"

"Do you notice how much healthier he is than all the other children?" my French wife frequently asks, referring to our current domicile of lard and polluted air. "He is doing much better than the statue quo . . . and eet is only because *I* am in charge of his health."

Health and food, in fact, are the subjects my French wife, much like my aging Jewish parents, can hold forth on for hours on end. They are, in fact, the only subjects which—genre-wise, if not in actual content—she shares with her biologically destined in-laws. "You have weak adrenals," she frequently tells me on the subject of my fatigue, "because of all your Jewish stress and your terrible diet. Just take a few of these," she pushes a pair of brindle-colored capsules my way, "for your adrenals, and a few of *these* to eliminate some of the free radicals in your blood system."

"What the hell are free radicals?" The expression makes me, a child of the '60s, think of the likes of Abby Hoffman, Bobby Seale, Eldridge Cleaver, and Huey Newton running amok among my red and white corpuscles.

"Too many unsaturated fats in your diet. Zee kind of things that come from too much of thees reheated oils and melted cheese that all zee junk foods you eat are so full of."

Much like the post office and the local police, my French wife keeps a kind of Most Wanted List of her most ardent undesirables. It goes something like this:

1. "Free Radicals"
2. Margarine
3. Store-bought tomatoes
4. Prescription drugs
5. Western medicine
6. Rancid fats
7. Processed cheese
8. Middle-class life
9. Money
10. Synthetic fibers

"Bless you, *mon amour*," I say. "I feel better already."

***

A French wife, if she's the product of relatively fertile ground, will provide you, not only with a half-French offspring and a French mother-in-law, but with a French brother-in-law and sister-in-law as well.

My brother-in-law, Marc Antoine, who lives in the

remote Hâutes-Alpes village of Montmorin (a town so devoid of inhabitants between the ages of six and sixty it had to advertise in the local paper for families with children to keep the school open) is a young man with what's called, in the vernacular of my native tongue, a loose wrist. Interspersed between the dozen-odd bottles of beer he inhales daily are likely to be found numerous glasses of *vin rouge*, an occasional cognac, shot of Calvados or *pasteque*, or—if the occasion calls for it—a dry martini. Yet, with the classical *panache* of the French, not a stutter enters into his step, not a slur passes over his lips, while I, his Jewish Gringo brother-in-law from the Promised Land, stagger among the homemade rooms of his stone house, drunk as a skunk on a single shot of Grand Marnier.

"Your brother sure can drink," I say to my French wife that night in bed. "*Everybody* zey can drink, Gringo," she replies, sipping on the beaker of Cointreau parked on the night table, "compared to you."

For my French sister-in-law, Annick (who resides in the relative metropolis of St. Etienne-les-Orgues (pop. 215) in the *marginaux*-infested *départment* of Alpes d'Hâute Provence some one-hundred kilometers southeast and whom I've nicknamed *"le lapin"*—the rabbit), it's not so much drinking that fills the interstices of the day as that other nemesis of the Puritanical American mind: fucking.

Dispersed like bird droppings throughout her little house, where Annick lives with her current lover, Thierry, and their three children (the youngest, Quentin, by him, the previous two, Marlon and Rudi, by one of her previous lovers, a seed-strewing young kleptomaniac by the name of Jean-Michel), the white plastic casings of various forms of French birth control and flavored condom wrappers illuminate the domestic landscape, filling my French wife and I with the kind of sexual jealousy and amazement only the married faced with the post-tumescent evidence of the still-inebriated know.

"My seester says even *she* sometimes wishes Thierry had a beet less energy," my wife tries to console me the night we arrive in St. Etienne, as I try to clear a path to our on-the-floor mattress through the Hansel-and-Gretel-like trail of sexual paraphernalia.

"I find that hard to believe," I say, trying to keep from laughing as the rafter beside our bed, impelled by the rhythmic swaying and moaning of Annick's and Thierry's bodies against the floorboards upstairs, gently sends my wife's *apératif* atrembling.

***

On the subject of money my French wife is, like many of the French I've met, a "spiritual person." In other words, though she's quite fond of *tendresse* in any way she can get it, she seems allergic to all forms of legal tend*er*, regardless of the currency in question.

"I theenk, Gringo," she suggested to me with a straight face shortly after unveiling the tombstone of her enormous debt, "we should send some money to those poor keeds at that *guarderia* in Ecuador."

"Ecuador?? Ecuador? Are you out of your fucking mind?" I suggested politely. "What about your poor husband right here in Cambridge onto whom you've just socked an unplanned-for child and $80,000 in debts he didn't know a fucking thing about?"

"You are deviating the conversation again," she replied calmly, her eyes sparkling like *crème brulée* in a *patisserie* window. "Zee fact is that we are much better off than almost zee whole rest of zee world . . . You need to have some sense of proportion, *mon amour*." In moments of discord, my French wife doesn't hesitate to resort to the ambiguous balm of terms of endearment right out of the worst of French sentimental movies. "Just because you have chosen thees empty American bourgeois life for yourself, eet doesn't mean zat I have to accept eet."

"Have you ever heard of *making* money, rather than *giving* it away?" I ask, a sense what I believe the French refer to as *sang-froid* beginning to crawl through my body.

"I am more interested, Gringo," she replies, "een my quality of life."

"Een thees country," I say, mimicking her accent, "you can't *have* a quality of life by squeezing essential oils from herbs or growing organic tomatoes, een case you haven't noticed."

"Oh, Gringo," says my French wife, "where is the romantic poet I met in Ecuador?"

The romantic poet my French wife met in Ecuador was never a man who had planned, for the second straight time, to marry a woman who thought of money as the root of all evil, or that a savings bank was a little 2" x 4" dollop of space located under her pillow.

"Did you know that all of the greatest writers," I inquire of her one night over dinner, "were solid members of the bourgeoisie?"

"What about Rimbaud?" she asks, exhibiting a rare moment of French patriotism.

"He quit writing at nineteen, and died not long thereafter."

"And Baudelaire?"

"He died young too, before he could get sensible enough to *want* to be a bourgeois."

"And ees that what *you* want?" asks my French wife.

"Oui, chéri," I say, *"c'est ça que je veux."*

My French wife is having one of her better days reinventing

the English language.

"It is better," she says to our eight-year-old son, who has spent the whole afternoon watching baseball on TV, "to live a full life than to be a potato couch." One of the Houston Astros has just hit what my wife, clearly not an *aficionado* of the sport, calls "a run home."

"Couch potato," I correct her, trying hard to keep a straight face.

"Couch potato, potato couch—either way, it's a potato and a couch, no?" she says.

"Yes," I concede. "Either way it's a potato and a couch."

"And, anyway," my wife adds, "he should not be sitting there like a potato couch, but should be working on his school project for Black Month History."

"Black History Month," I correct her again, ever gently.

"Oh, *merde*," says my wife, "Black History Month, Black Month History—why does this crazy country of yours have so many bloody holidays?

Later that afternoon, we take our son to the local Deep Eddy pool, where my wife has yet another novel idea. "Let's play Middle in the Monkey," she suggests.

My son, who's been getting hip to his mother's unusual way with—no pun intended—his mother tongue, cracks up. "*Monkey* in the *Middle!*" he wails into the early spring air.

"What's the difference?" says my wife, beginning to look fatigued. "There's a monkey, there's a middle—who cares what order zey're in?"

"And now," my French wife says, as our poolside afternoon draws to a close, "I suppose we must go to Rib's Art House."

"Art's Rib House," I correct her, trying hard to hold it in. "They serve *ribs* there, not art."

"*Pour moi,*" my wife, apparently not all that humored by her own string of *faux pas*, "I would prefer to go somewhere where they serve art—those ribs are full of grease and cholesterol from pigs fed with chemicals. And anyway," she continues, "I have so many things to do at home—I must, for example, install the new lightning in the bathroom . . . or do you think, *peut-être*, that the light comes from out of space?"

"You don't by any chance mean *outer* space, do you?"

"Out of space, outer space—*qu'est-ce la différence?*" Possessed of a talent to rival the great trade unionists with a screwdriver, saw, and electric drill, you might say my French wife is a tad less accomplished in the world of speech.

"Congratulations on your reward, *mon amour*," she greets me the afternoon I've gotten word of having received a prize for my novel. "I married a genius."

I wish I had, too . . . or at least someone who speaks English, I mutter under my breath, informing her that a reward is something you get for returning a lost pet or providing a tip to the police on the whereabouts of a suspected axe murderer.

"Eeet is so confusing, zee English language," she says sweetly, smiling her most innocent French smile. "I'm afraid sometimes I wheel never learn it."

"*Moi aussi,*" I reply, tipping my Boston Red Sox cap and doing my best imitation of Maurice Chevalier, "*moi aussi*, I am afraid."

My French wife is also planning to have the "exhaustion pipe" replaced on our car, and the "shoe brakes" as well. I'm not sure whether the former is also an oblique reference to our sex life, or whether she's referring only to the car, but, either way, it seems to me improvements might be made, and I don't hesitate to say so.

"I feel samewise," says my French wife.

"You mean likewise," I say.

"Likewise, samewise," she answers. "It's all the same to me."

"Don't you sometimes wish you were married to someone who understood your jokes?" my friend Richard, married to a lovely mathematician from Tennessee, asks.

"Hell no," I answer. "My wife's English *is* a joke."

In the midst of all these linguistic and mechanical machinations, my French wife seems determined to keep our domestic and culinary life on an even keel, led by her universally acclaimed *tarte aux pommes* and *soupe aux pistoux*. Yet, quite emphatically, she doesn't intend to grow old in this great country of ours, with its infamous social safety net.

"I don't want to spend my last years in *a retiring home* in this country of yours," she informs me over one of her incomparable meals, "where all the men grow sick and fat, and all the women have cosmic surgery."

"I don't think you need to worry about it," I say. "I don't think so at all."

"This is the best apple tart in the world," my friend Ross, echoing a sentiment widespread among our friends, says. "The best fucking apple tart in the world."

"I made the crust myself," my French wife proudly informs him, "with a pinroll."

"You mean a rolling pin?" I try to help out.

"*Oui,* a roller pin," she stands corrected, nearly spitting out the words.

And it is no small thing, to be sure—this indescribable *tarte*. To do something so well, to make this widely acclaimed "best fucking apple tart in the world" (a sentiment in which our five-year-old son, with a resounding *"Maman, j'aime ça beaucoup,"* obviously concurs), is certainly a feat not to be taken lightly, or easily dismissed. Who, after all, is to say that my French wife, like William Carlos Williams before her, is not the happy genius of our household?

"'Je l'ai connu, moi, il etait intraitable, il vivait à Bologne avec deux soeurs, il ne sortait quasiment de chez lui que pour aller aux putes.'—Fort bien, repris-je, s'il avait besoin de ça pour peindre ensuite comme Vermeer et Chardin, bénies soient toutes les putes du ciel et de la terre. Amen." (I knew him, he was incurable, he lived in Bologne with his two sisters, and only left his house to go to the whores—all the better, I thought, if he had need of that in order to paint like Vermeer and Chardin, blessed be all the whores of heaven and earth.)

So writes the Portuguese poet Eugenio de Andrade, of a conversation with a friend about the Italian still-life painter Morandi, in a book of translations my friend Patrick has lent me—a book which I, in turn, have lent my French wife in order to momentarily deflect her dark humor on the subject of our starkly diminished sexual relations.

"What does he mean by *'aller aux putes'*?" I ask upon encountering the to-me-unfamiliar term.

"It means to go to the wars," my French wife explains.

I'm momentarily befuddled, having always thought of Morandi as a more or less peace-loving sort of fellow.

"You mean as in *la guerre*?"

"No, Gringo, I mean like in going to a prostitute—*une poule.*"

"You mean *whores.*"

"Yes, that's what I said—wars."

I take a deep breath. I sigh into the sheets. Nonetheless,

she bakes, my French wife, the best fucking apple tart in the world.

Three/Trois

To say that my French wife is an ectomorph would be to expose oneself as a master of understatement. My wife's body, to describe the situation more accurately, could turn the average anorexic green with envy: She is, to say the least, rather thin.

"Oh, you are so wonderfully *slim*," many another woman, robust with the fleshliness that drives men wild, will say to her at a party, a compliment which might be translated, in the pre-feminist vernacular, as "I wish all these men would quit staring at *my* ass and look at *yours* for awhile, babycakes."

"Bones," I remark one night to my Hungarian mistress, a healthy, meat-eating alternative to my French wife, "are for dogs. Flesh is for humans. There's all the time in the world in the next life to spend with bones."

"You weren't this thin when I met you," I complain to my wife.

"I wasn't thees *unhappy* when you met me either, Gringo," she accuses back.

"Your wife," a man says to me at a New Year's Eve party, grabbing his date by the ass, "is so beautifully thin."

"Yes," I say. "She's French. They eat like birds."

"As long as they make you sing," he smiles, "I suppose that's okay."

"Do I look like someone who's singing?" I ask.

My French wife, nonetheless, has a beautiful, soulful face. The kind of face that connoisseurs of *la différence* refer to as sensual, rather than sexy. The kind of face you can imagine being equally aroused by having its lips up against a wheel of brie or a widgeon of camembert as against the meatier protrusions of a male member.

"I love *good* food," my wife perpetually reminds me when we are forced into a comparison of appetites, "and you just love food."

"She is a very spiritual person, your wife, no?" a colleague asks me one night at a party.

"Yes," I say, nodding my head like someone acknowledging a death in the family, "*elle est une femme très spirituelle*. And I, alas, am a fallen angel."

***

My French wife is also inordinately fond of sending *"gros bisoux"* to her relatives on the telephone, at roughly sixty-five cents per minute.

"Au revoir, Maman," she says. *"Je te donne un gros bisou."*

Un gros bisou is a kiss—a BIG kiss, which is to say, coming from the lips of the French, that it's a helluva kiss indeed . . . a helluva LONG kiss, that is, if you're the one paying the phone bill.

The French, as you may know if you've ever been to France, love to kiss. They kiss everywhere and everyone—at least once on each cheek, and, if you're from a family like my wife's, twice . . . which makes four kisses per person in all. Walk into a room full of people with anyone from my wife's family, and what that translates into is a good three-quarters of an hour spent just brushing your lips up against other people's stubble and mascara.

The in-person kisses I don't like, but *les gros bisoux aux telefon* simply drive me crazy. *"Je te donne un gros bisou,"* my wife, courtesy of MTI, says to her mother, followed shortly by a variety of puckering sounds . . . in French, of course. *"Au revoir, maman, je te donne un gros bisou,"* she repeats. More puckering sounds. *"Un gros bisou,"* she then adds, as though the words had never before been uttered, and then—as if, by changing the word order, the message itself could become, like Christ on Mount Tabor, transmogrified: *"un gros bisou, maman."*

I, while all this *bisou*ing and *mama*ing are going on, am seated on the living room sofa, my thoughts on the phone bill, breathing deeply.

"Don't you *ever* again do that when I am talking to my mother!" my wife, who hardly ever raises her French voice, shouts at me after—at least a half-dozen *bisoux* and *au revoir mamans* later—she finally gets off the phone.

"Do what?"

"Seet there making deep breaths when I am on the phone with my mother."

I look up. "For what all those *bisoux* and *je t'embrasses* add to the phone bill, chèrie," I say, "you could fly to France."

***

We've moved to Texas, and my French wife—get this—actually *likes* it there. Unhappy about the unripe tomatoes and pompous intellectuals of Cambridge, not wild about the Jews in Israel, she seems to have suddenly taken to, of all things, refugee Texans from the '60s with their hair in ponytails, tattoos on their thighs and rings through their noses. (My French wife, I have always suspected, is a closet hippie, a—as she likes to describe her family and friends in the South of France—true *marginaux* at heart.)

I, on the other hand, am not *marginaux* at all . . . I aspire, in fact, to being kind of in the mainstream, a member of the solid bourgeoisie *à la* Thomas Mann and William Styron. As for rings, I don't even much like them on my fingers, much less through my nose, ears, navels, and various other parts of the anatomy our

Texas neighbors seem to like to put them through. But, for my French wife at least, anything—repeat, *anything*—is better than being surrounded by a bunch of "intellectuals," people who know nothing about essential oils or bamboo.

In Texas, my French wife has even been able to find her perfect tomato . . . or (of course) a loaf of bread satisfying to her simple-but-discerning French palate.

Now it is November, a month when even the Texas weather begins to send a not-so-soft chill through her fragile French bones. I am driving her and my son to the airport. In merely a matter of hours, she will be holding in her delicate but strong hands the perfect tomato, a loaf of irreplaceable—and inimitable—French bread. Delta Flight #1620 is soon to leave for Cincinnati. Then, *Grace à Dieux*, my strange little bi-national twosome will switch to—you guessed it!—AIR FRANCE (where the food is real, the newspaper *Le Monde*, and the language *le vrai français*).

Tomorrow, my French wife and half-French son will awake in *la belle France*.

***

My French wife returns from France three weeks later, on Thanksgiving night ("Thanksgiving," she says, "has no meaning for zee French") to be precise, with three kinds of paté—*paté de truffe* (truffles), *délice d'oie* (goose), and *paté du lapin* (rabbit)—and—*grâce à Dieu*—a new, genuinely French, broom. *"Thees,"* she says, waving a bright blue mass of something vaguely resembling punk-dyed horsehairs in my face, "is a *real* broom." It *is*, in fact, a real broom, and—just like a new broom should—it sweeps clean.

The paté, too, is good: It is *real* paté, and I, who have just gotten the latest high-cholesterol report back from my doctor, try—sipping a bit of real French *vin rouge* en route—to be grateful. In fact, I *am* grateful: After all, I have a French wife, a French broom, an uncircumcised half-French son, and—what's more—some *genuine* French paté.

***

It's no small thing, my son and I soon discover, to teach a French wife the rules of baseball.

"The man with the bat and the man catching zee ball," she asks. It's the Red Sox, my son's favorite team, against the Yankees. "Are zey on the same team?"

"No, chèrie," I explain. "The catcher is on the same team as the *pitcher*, and the pitcher, and catcher are both trying to get the batter *out*."

"Then why doesn't he *swing* at the ball when the pitcher throws it?"

"He's waiting for a good pitch," explains my son.

"So that he can heet a run home?"

"A home run," I correct her.

"*Oui,* a home run . . . But then there will be a run home, so *qu'est que la différence?*"

"No big deal, I suppose," I admit.

"And why, sometimes, are zey running around the field, and sometimes zey are walking?"

"Because, sometimes, the batter walks, but then—if he hits the ball—he's supposed to *run* around the bases."

"It is much easier, *je pense*," says my wife, "to understand *boules*. In zat game, *nobody* is in a hurry, and they are not spending all their time running and walking between pillows."

***

My French wife, ever obsessed with issues of health, scours the neighborhood for discarded furniture, which she will then proceed to "recuperate." I try to convince her of the fact that, while these pieces may well be damaged, they are by no standard—either French or American—diseased.

"Refurbish, chérie," I try and correct her, "you are going to *refurbish* these pieces—or, at least, *refinish* them . . . But furniture, I'm afraid, simply cannot be recuperated."

"Why not?" she insists. "They look sick to me. And, when I am finished with them, they will look well. *Dans mon pays*, at least, we call this "recuperate.""

How to argue with such logic, I wonder. Or, for that matter, with such a recuperating spirit, so unlike my own.

***

"You are," my French wife says when I return home from the super-market with—on sale, of course—four *Balsen* chocolate marble cakes . . . *bester Deutsche qualitat*, "a chronicle case."

"Are you, *chèrie,* accusing me of being a magazine?" I reply, amused *comme d'habitude.*

"You know what I mean," she insists. "You have a chronicle sugar problem. I am sitting here baking cakes with organic ingre-dients and very little sugar, and you go out to the supermarket and bring home this *garbàge,* full of rancid fats and free radicals."

***

"Felicitations, Monsieur Weinstock," the voice on our American-made answering machine—a *real* French voice—congratulates me when I arrive home some days later. *"Je suis heureux de vous informer que vous êtes devenu citoyen de la France."*

For several years now—from Budapest to Haifa, from Haifa to Texas—my wife has been manically trying to claim for me my marital dowry rights, as *père de famille*, to become a citizen of *la belle France.* And now, finally, according to the cheery, congratulatory *voix douce* of Madame Sauvagny of the French Consulate in Houston, she has succeeded, or so boldly proclaims the significant seeming 8 ½" X 11" diploma like document that arrives in our mailbox the following week, bearing Dossier no. 1996DX010997

RÉPUBLIQUE FRANÇAISE

Pár déclaration
Souscrite le: 02/07/1996
devant: **l'Ambassade de la France en/au HONGIRE**
enregistrée sou le numéro: **07624/97**
en application de l'article 21-2 du Code Civil
A acquis la nationalité française:
WEINSTOCK Martin Charles
Né le 08/03/1949 VINELAND (ÉTATS UNIS)
La Ministre de l'Emploi et de la Solidarité
Martine AUBRY

And there—voila!—it is: I, Charles Martin Weinstock of Austin, Texas, formerly Martin Charles Weinstock of Vineland, New Jersey, and Washington Heights, New York, am now, as Yeats would put it, "transformed, transformed utterly." And if it's not exactly a terrible beauty that it is born, it is certainly something not quite resembling what I once thought of as me: Now, by a fell swoop of my French wife's dogged determination and the lackadaisical pen of *Monsieur Martine Aubry, Ministre de l'Emploi et de la Solidarité,* I am, like Christ atop Mount Tabor, transmogrified: I am now *"M. Charles Weinstock, Citoyen de la République Française."*

"Okay *mon amour*," my French wife says. "Let's lift a glass of champagne to your becoming French."

La jour de gloire est, indeed, *arrivée:* My French wife, finally, has a French husband.

***

"Do you think we should go on living together, or should we divorce?" my French wife brings up the "d" word one night over dinner. We're having a pizza (she *hates* melted cheese) at the local *Okay Italia*, the legs and mini-skirt capital of Budapest, where the only thing between you and your waitress's pudenda is your sense of decorum, and your waning ideals concerning fidelity.

Sometimes I, too, think of divorcing my French wife. Sometimes I've had enough of the "statue quo." Sometimes I've had enough of playing "middle in the monkey," of being a "potato couch." If I'm going to have to listen to a foreign language, I sometimes wish it weren't my own. And, after all, how long can an aging Jewish American boy like me stand to be married to someone from a country that considers homeopathy one of the world's major religions, work a capitalist conspiracy, circumcision a barbarian ritual, and picnics one of life's major spiritual events?

But, of course, questions like this, though they may have everything to do with literature, have little, if anything, to do with marriage. When you add it all up (which we rarely, if ever, actually do), she's a lovely girl, my French wife.

Why, I might even marry her again.

TOMORROW

The renowned historian, plump with dollar bills and fired up by Viagra, had seemed a good catch at first. Though eighty-one, he was still publishing and lecturing actively, and, having survived three wives, was now living alone, surrounded by his collection of antique Herend vases and Fauvist paintings, on his two-hundred-acre estate in the foothills of the Poconos, from where he commuted twice weekly to teach a graduate seminar in Central European History at the University of Pennsylvania.

Though his performance in bed could hardly compete with what she had known in her younger days, she realized that there, too, there was nothing to complain about. Put it this way: He at least performed. Which is more than could be said about many of the men she had known who were two-thirds his age.

A youthful sixty-two, she had hesitated at first at the thought of being with a so much older man. Her last lover, a painter with whom she had lived for twenty years before he left her for an eighteen-year-old student of his, had been a full ten years younger than she was.

But that, she now realized, had been another time, another body.

She and the historian had met in Budapest at a cocktail party following a lecture he had delivered at the Central European University on the subject of Roosevelt, Churchill and Stalin's meeting at Yalta, a historical event he insisted had been preceded by secret agreements that rendered the actual summit something of a charade. Though she herself was not much interested in history—her own passions ran primarily in the areas of painting, music and poetry—a friend had insisted she come along and, lonely amid the waning November light of Andrassy út, she somewhat reluctantly agreed to do so. The lecture, however, had been interesting enough, and she had to admit that the lecturer, in a bright blue spotted bow tie and lavender shirt, seemed a good deal more sprightly and animated than she assumed a man his age was entitled to be.

"He's quite a charmer, old Tibor, just you wait and see," Zsuzsa had said over a latté at the Müvesz Café before the lecture. "Who knows—maybe *you'll* even fall for him!"

She doubted it, not being much in the mood for either romance or love. Her love life, she had figured, was most probably over by now. She had her dog, her country house in the Hungarian *puszta*, her poetry, her painting, her memories. What more could a woman entering into the onset of her dotage expect?

But there she was, at the reception following the lecture, and there he was, standing beside her, sweeping her off her feet with his perfect Hungarian. Várady, a post-1956 escapee from Hungary who spoke an elegant and Old World *magyarul*, had devoted all the available charm he could muster over a glass of 1998 Villányi Kekfrankos to arrange for a private dinner between the two of them at Gundel's, Budapest's best-known, and most expensive, restaurant. Hardly having the kind of budget that could afford Gundel's on her own, and well enough outfitted for the occasion in the backless red dress she had, perhaps in anticipation, chosen for the evening—she said yes. The dog's walk, after all, could wait.

The charm offensive had continued on through dinner, and then into the next day during a walk on Margaret Island, when she, a devout Jungian, discovered the most amazing of synchronicities: Her companion had been born, some forty years before the momentous event itself, in very same house on Délibáb utca where she, then a vivacious young university student, had lost her virginity!

While they stopped for an ice cream at the Margaret Island Radisson, Tibor suggested she come visit him, all expenses paid, in Pennsylvania, that spring. She had been to the States on several occasions with her painter ex-husband—always to New York—but everyone had always told her that "New York isn't America," and the chance to see the real thing—and, what's more, at the historian's expense—was hardly an unattractive offer. So, sealed with a kiss, she agreed to go.

Like many a Magyar male, Tibor Várady had been for many a ride on the carousel of love: three wives, a series of mistresses, and an eye for women that refused to linger for all too long in a single place. Though hardly breathtakingly attractive himself—he had developed a considerable paunch over his fourscore years, and a rather puffy, reddish face to go with it—he was one of those men whose self-confidence and sense of his own limitless charms seemed to more than compensate for a lack of the actual qualities that might have merited them. Women, those strangest and most alluring of creatures, seemed drawn to him nonetheless.

"Be careful," Zsuzsa had warned her before her departure, "the old codger still has quite the reputation." Judging from the leisure reading volumes she found at his house once she arrived in

Pennsylvania, Zsuzsa seemed to be right. His favorite, of which he owned multiple copies, was a modern classic entitled *In Praise of Older Women: The Amorous Recollections of A. V.*, by Stephen Vizinczey, a book he claimed to have re-read a dozen times, and that famously began, "I was born into a devout Roman Catholic family, and spent a great part of my first ten years among kindly Franciscan monks." Tibor, too, had been born into a devout Roman Catholic family, though he had done without the monks. He had done without older women as well: his preference, she could tell from the countless photos mounted on the walls and bookshelves, had always run to the significantly younger sort.

Anna was no stranger to the slings and arrows of love herself. Breathtakingly beautiful as a young girl in Debrecen, she had married—shortly after losing her virginity on Délibáb utca—for the first time at eighteen, given birth before she was twenty-three to two now-grown children, divorced at twenty-five, remarried at twenty-seven, and lost her second husband, an architect whom she adored and was, for the most part, faithful to, just two years later when his car stalled at a railroad crossing in Debrecen just before the guardrail had come down. It was, to say the least, not a pretty death.

She now gazed at herself, naked, in the mirror. They had all begun to droop: breasts, buttocks, thighs, even, she had to confess, spirit. There was no way to deny it: she was not what she once had been. But the house was lovely, as was the lay of the land, the hills of Pennsylvania, birds one could never have imagined in Budapest or Kecskemét, or even along the *puszta*. Tibor had a wonderful collection of wines, a concert Steinway (which the first of his three wives had played professionally), an art collection that would have been the envy of many a small museum. He was a worldly, sophisticated man who he seemed utterly enamored with her. What more could she ask for?

Yet the twenty-year difference in age between them and what it boded for the future rarely left her thoughts. Someday, if things went as the actuarial tables indicated they would, she would be queen of all this. She would be like Marie Theresa in the foothills of the Poconos: This could be *her* Gödöllo, she its Sisi. And, what's more, she *liked* him. Perhaps—who knew?—it could even develop into that thing called love. But she had been *there* before, and it was not, she thought to herself, a place she was all that eager to revisit.

But this time, even at their ripe and advanced age, she thought, things might be different.

***

They had agreed, at her insistence, on two ceremonies. The first—a religious service, mostly for the benefit of her friends and remaining family—would take place in Kecskemét at the baroque Old Catholic Church (her mother had been a Catholic, her father a Calvinist), designed by an eighteenth-century Piarist father, Oszwald Gáspár. She had always loved wandering near it as a child, gazing at its façade decorated with reliefs commemorating the Seventh William Hussars and local heroes of the War of Independence. After the service, there would be dinner at the cozy *Kecskemét Csárda* (she herself would have preferred the classier *Geniusz* nearby, which offered slightly more international fare with a French twist, but it was, after all, *he* who was paying, and the entire ceremony, she reasoned with herself, had been *her* idea).

The second ceremony, a month later, would take place at his house in Pennsylvania. His four children from his previous marriages, of course, would be there and, no doubt, several of his former mistresses, now disguised as friends. But that, she figured, was the way things went when one married again late in life: you accepted the terrain as it was, weeds, stumps and all. After all, at their age, *everyone* was entitled to a past, weren't they?

She had gone by taxi—a rare extravagance for someone on her tight budget—to pick him up at the airport when he arrived in early April for the first of their two nuptials. The cherry trees had already begun to blossom in Budapest—it was an unusually early spring—and she could occasionally see storks flying overhead en route to their usual summer nesting places atop village chimneys. The Budapest Spring Festival was also about to begin and, with it, the usual season of political intrigue and false promises from Left to Right. Everything spoke, for better and worse, of new beginnings: air of expectancy reigned all around her.

When he emerged into the terminal at Ferihegy 2, she had noticed something a bit more distant than usual in his demeanor— his habitually demonstrative greeting to her whenever they were re-united seemed, on this occasion, a bit lukewarm. She consoled herself by attributing it to the expectable nervousness of a man about to be married for the fourth time. In the backseat of the cab on the way back to her—actually *their*—apartment (though it had been paid for mostly with his money), he had withdrawn his hand from hers several times when she tried to grasp it.

"Is something the matter?" she had asked.

"No," he replied, looking away as he spoke. "I'm just nervous about having to finish the galleys for my new book . . . there's so much yet to do."

Ah, academics, she thought to herself. How reluctantly the life of the mind gave itself over to the life of the body—or, for that matter, to celebration of any sort. Her first husband had been a painter, her long-time younger lover a writer: artists were little better. She herself, a minor practitioner of the three great arts (painting, poetry, music), could well relate to the problem of divided attentions, but, with Tibor at least, she had found herself, much to her own delight, dwelling more than usually in the present.

That night they didn't make love, a rare event for his seemingly perpetually youthful, albeit chemically revivified, libido. He was tired, he said, it had been a long flight. They would have plenty of time to make up for it, she replied, tomorrow they would be man and wife.

The next morning, on the way to Kecskemét for the ceremony, they sat in the backseat once more, while her son and daughter-in-law sat in the front. Tibor still seemed rather distant and subdued, but the wedding itself, a purely religious ceremony with no binding civil function, went without a hitch. She couldn't help noticing how dashing, for a man of almost eighty-one, he was, nor that he seemed hardly impervious to the charms and allures of the various young bridesmaids and other female guests among the assembled. His gaze, she noticed, especially for a man who was about to be married, hardly ever met hers. The seal of his wedding kiss seemed to be made of a glue that was not certain to hold.

After the ceremony, and then after dinner, there was a great deal of dancing and—it was, after all, Hungary—*drinking* at the Csárda. Tibor's air of distraction and distance seemed to abate somewhat under the influence of several *pálinkas* and a shared bottle of the finest champagne. He would be leaving again the very next morning—"inflexible professional obligations," as he had explained it—and they would not be seeing each other again until the second ceremony in Pennsylvania a month later. *That* one would seal their union, not only in the eyes of God, but in the merely mortal and ever-wavering gaze of man.

The days, the hours, the minutes had flown by since the morning of the church ceremony in Kecskemét, and it was now the day before her departure for Pennsylvania, with so much packing and cleaning and putting things in order yet to do. The apartment near the City Park was marvelously spacious and well lit, and she reflected, as she placed a recording of the pianist András Schiff playing Bach onto the CD player, on how truly fortunate she was—a woman nearing the upper end of mid-age who had hardly any money of her own and, yet, three such beautiful residences (she had purchased the summer house near the banks of the Tisza River decades ago with her former husband) in which to occupy herself.

Though somewhat nervous about her forthcoming half-life in America—she thought of her English as, at best, marginal, and considered the country itself, with its excessive extroversion and lack of any substantial history, a rather superficial place—it all seemed exquisitely bountiful to her when she considered where she had been only months earlier. She thought of herself as a woman, for the most part, blessed by fate.

True, Tibor had been more than a little distant since, and leading up to, that day in Kecskemét. But in just three days all that would change once more: A real American minister, vested with the authority of both church *and* state, would pronounce them man and wife, until death did them part.

She had called Tibor last night—a conversation punctuated, as had more and more frequently become the case, by long silences on his normally garrulous part—and she hung up the phone feeling disturbed and uneasy. Now, a bevy of black crows were squawking on the plane tree outside the bedroom window, and she resolved to spend this, her last day as a single woman, listening to the music she most loved—Kodaly, Bartok, Liszt, Kurtag, Ligeti (the latter two personal friends), and, of course, Bach and Mozart—and treating herself to a soothing medicinal bath at the nearby Széchenyi Fürdo. The entrance fee of 1,500 forints was a luxury that, in her single life, she could rarely afford, but all that, too, was soon to change: For someone of Tibor's wealth and background, it was, as he himself liked to put it (an Americanism she very much liked), "a drop in the bucket."

She tenderly caressed her dog, Lutza, who, alas, would not be coming with her, but would be staying with her son and daughter-in-law nearby. Lutza had been a good and devoted companion to her in her loneliness, and it saddened her to think that, in exchange for a mere husband, she would have to at least partially give up the companionship of so loving and unconditionally devoted a creature. But *az élet nem hobostorta*, as the Hungarians liked to say: Life was not a cream cake. There were, in all venues, compromises to be made.

"I'm a bit worried about this Tibor of yours," Zsuzsa, who had by now become a kind of Cassandra in her eyes, remarked as they sat in the thirty-five-degree centigrade basin of the Széchenyi. "He behaved very strangely indeed at your wedding—why, he hardly even looked you in the eyes!" Yes, it had indeed been so— she herself hadn't failed to notice—but she had attributed it mainly to what she by now considered a lifelong, near-pathological fear of intimacy on the part of *all* men. And what, after all could be more threatening from the point of view of intimacy than one's own wedding?

"I'm not worried about it," she consoled both Zsuzsa and herself, trying to make light of her own concerns. "He'll get over it—he's still young."

She had already crawled into bed—it had been a long, hard, emotionally exhausting day, music and all—and was just turning off the light from having read the Rilke's love poems to God from *The Book of Hours*, when the phone rang. She gazed at the clock: 11:15 p.m. It was often at around this time that Tibor called—she usually stayed up late reading and writing—but he hadn't, for some reason, called for several days now, though she had left several messages on his answering machine before finally having reached him last night.

But now she was tired: all the packing and anticipation, along with the uneasiness implanted in her by Zsuzsa's dark premonitions, had taken its toll. For some reason she couldn't quite place, she didn't, now, feel like talking to him . . . and who else could it be at this hour? She wanted, for the moment, to be alone with her dreams, and with her thoughts.

She decided not to answer, preferring to go to sleep with her fantasies intact, undisturbed even by the sound of her husband's voice. They would have plenty of time to talk once she got off the plane in Pittsburgh. Whatever it was he had to tell her could surely wait until tomorrow.

GOOD NIGHT AND GOOD LUCK

Those days, Weinstock realized now, had been precious—the going to sleep at the hour he chose and rising in the same manner, the bucolic early-morning swims in the lake, with no one else there but the occasional aging widow determined to keep up her tan and stay in shape. Hope, he realized, springs eternal, even if it usually proves false.

Now his wife and sister-in-law, and his sister-in-law's young son Raphael, were with him, and, pleasant as it was to have company for dinner and someone else to work in the garden, and on the myriad tasks that needed to be done in and around the house with, it was no longer the solitary and entirely self-generated life he had grown used to during the past weeks. His time, his days—his life, in other words—were no longer entirely his own.

He had found, recently, that—just as desire had been the main concern of the first half (he assumed, in a rare instance of current optimism, that it would prove to be only the first half) of his earthly existence—it was now, more and more, the diminution and end of desire that were his subjects, and, the more they became so, the more consoling—indeed, tranquilizing—he found their repercussions to be. *What makes the engine go?* the old poet had written—*desire, desire, desire.* But perhaps it was the *end* of desire, too, that could make the engine go . . . if not at the same speed, then at least on a smoother course.

And as for others—well, there was some re-thinking to be done there too. Perhaps, he now thought, *people who need people,* to quote that notable American poet, Barbra Streisand, *weren't* the luckiest people in the world: Perhaps people who *didn't* need them, a population he increasingly found himself among, were far luckier still.

All these ruminations lingered within him as he rose, exhausted from once again sleeping beside his wife, and went for his morning swim in Lake Balaton—the water a chilling nineteen degrees centigrade, the sun a bright yellow globe in the morning sky, the air brisk and revivifying. Today, unlike the usual family of two parents and seven little ones he saw on his morning swim, there had been only a solitary swan in the lake. Who knew? Perhaps it, too, was trying to reclaim its solitude.

As a young man, he had always sided, the best evidence notwithstanding, with the optimists—those cheerful purveyors of uplifting scenarios and high spirits, the Bill Clintons and Barack Obamas as opposed to the Robert Doles and John McCains. But, increasingly, the words of the retired schoolteacher from Charlotte, North Carolina his friend Rob often cast in his documentaries came back to him, "Listen, Rob, it's *all* a tragedy, so the best we can do is grin and bear it and make the most of it and get on with our day."

Yes, increasingly it *did* all seem like a tragedy—his sister dead of cancer just two weeks ago, his wife's sexual allure, at least in the eyes of his often misdirected libido, roughly the equivalent of that of the moles who, at this very moment, were decimating his yard, his son picking away daily at the large, now infected, pimple on his nose, and his own skin, he had to confess, suffering from more than its share of bumps and protrusions, of scar tissue and incipient inflammations.

Indeed, one of the few remaining joys he could truly count on amidst his quotidian meanderings was that of picking things—dead skin, congealed mucous, flaky ear wax, bellybutton lint, dried post-masturbatory semen—from his own body, a joy he attributed in part to the natural pleasures of self-dismemberment and, partly, to the hope for renewal and replacement each such removal fed upon, and aroused.

He wondered, in fact, how politicians and public figures— those with cameras and notepads constantly pointed at them— could tolerate the lack of opportunity for such private pleasures that must accompany their ever-public condition. *What a drag!* he thought to himself, freshly consoled by, and resigned to, his own anonymity and obscurity.

In any event, here he was: a ripe, un-libidinal fifty-eight, a man whose only present reason for putting his hands in his pocket were to have them emerge, later, holding some spare change. *Change me! Change me!* The Woman at the Washington Zoo had inveighed, but why, really, bother? Would it *really* be so exciting now, at this late date, to change?

No. Self-acceptance, he realized, was going to be more up his alley. He could, after all, still emerge as a kind of Kierkegaardian knight of resignation, a man from whom the first thing that rose in the morning was not his pecker, but his hopes for a lower cholesterol count and a good rare hamburger. After all, as his oldest friend, Donald Wellbright, Distinguished Professor of Existentialism and Phenomenology (two disciplines, he was once certain, that had died along with his mother in the late 1960s) at the University of Chicago had once written to him, *"I have come to believe that the category of erotic error is one of the fundamental ones in his life and in the life of a very few people I know. You're one of them."*

Et voilà, there it was! He was one of them. Erotic error was what he was now being saved from, so why not just chin up and enjoy it? Would he *really* be better off temporarily revivified by Viagra and Cialis, eternally fearful of that four-hour-long erection that would send him and his latest erotic mistake racing off to the local emergency room? He hardly thought so.

Better, he reckoned, to make one's peace with whatever waxing (ears included) and waning life offered and thank whoever might be up there, if not for his unconquerable soul, then at least for the fortitude of his now-resigned equanimity. He had played Henry Miller for long enough, most assuredly, and Charles Bukowski as well. Big deal, if he was now little more than a mercilessly ill-clad and sexlessly gnome-like Eckhart Tolle?

Wisdom is learning what to overlook, one of his favorite poets, *The Woman at the Washington Zoo* man, had written, and if that, indeed, was wisdom, who was to say that he wasn't growing wise? If hell, indeed, was other people, as another ugly little gnome, that French toad Sartre, had suggested, then wasn't heaven, perhaps, the lack of them? Certainly it was a possibility worth contemplating. Maybe better, like his dear friend Rita, to run off to South Africa and live with the baboons—*they*, at least, as she was so eager to point out, didn't have a language to lie with. Or, for that matter, any lies worth telling.

Of course, occasionally a little youthful rambunctiousness still descended upon him—clitoris and vulva, anus and orifice—all those would again begin to seem, albeit temporarily, like lovely words. But that, too, would fade, as would his morning erection, and the force that through the green fuse drove the flower would relocate into his fingertips and onto the computer keyboard.

Mirabile dictu, as the saying goes. Sometimes the staggering flesh merely deposits itself in a merciful way, and we emerge, full of awe and wonder, to find yet another page has been filled without the unnecessary spilling of seed. Demonstrations abound of aging satyrs who have founded, not only their own pontificates, but entire colonies of streaming disciples, eager to take the same vows of abstinence and drive whatever remains of mercy home through their own fingertips.

"Only when you fuck is everything that you dislike in life and everything by which you are defeated in life purely, if momentarily, revenged," one of his earliest heroes, Philip Roth, had written. "Only then are you most cleanly alive and most cleanly yourself. Yes, sex too is limited in its power. I know how very well limited. But tell me, what power is greater?"

Well, now maybe he *could* tell him: *No sex* was the power that was greater than sex. No sex—and no desire for it, either—could beat sex nine times out of ten. No sex, he realized, was his revenge against revenge. It was cleaner, safer, tidier and more honest than sex could ever be. He could imagine now, even, something he would once have found unimaginable: an erotics of kindness—after all, given how little kindness there truly *was* in the world, wasn't there something erotic, even illicit, about it?

Many years ago, an acquaintance he had met at a writer's conference, an aging professor of aesthetics from Washington University in St. Louis, had confessed to him that one of the major sources of his relative contentment with life was that he was someone virtually devoid of erotic desire. Two weeks later, however, he left his wife for a thirty-year-younger woman, a sex bomb from the East Village covered with indiscreetly suggestive tattoo art whose major allure, Weinstock speculated, could not possibly have been her acquaintance with the collected works of Suzanne Langer. If there was anyone up there, as Weinstock obsessively speculated there must be, He or She mostly certainly had a sense of humor . . . of that, at least, he was sure.

Weinstock, to be frank, had had a pretty good life thus far. There had been women, openly and in selected discrete liaisons, there had been travel, life in foreign countries, the company of Nobel Prize winners and Supreme Court Justices, even, occasionally, enthusiastic audiences of his own. Among the world's legions of the sick, hungry, deprived and miserable, his, to be sure, was a relatively benign fate. He woke to sleep, and took his waking slow.

Even now, there were still moments of adventure— without, even, the benign chemical intervention of Viagra or Cialis. What was ordained to rise, when it had to, still went up, though it endured a far more precipitous, and hasty, fall when the time came for it to be overtaken by boredom, or by sleep.

The other night, for example, Weinstock found himself in the company of a long-legged, 5' 11" beauty, the direct descendant of the Mayflower pilgrims, a designer of high-end bed and bathroom tiles whose mosaics had graced, among other places, the bathroom of the Queen of England and kitchen counter top of Madonna. She had even designed her own tasteful, if not entirely spacious, living room sofa, upon which their Saturday evening liaison, while not entirely reaching its desired dénouement, was, for the most part, satisfactorily concluded. She and Weinstock hadn't known much about one another when the evening commenced, and, by the time it was over, knew only a little bit more, but it seemed more than enough for them both. There was after all, only so much a man his age could still take, or give, and perhaps a woman as well.

Weinstock was a lawyer in a small to medium sized firm specializing in personal injury cases and malpractice. The assorted malfeasances of others, in other words, were his bread and butter . . . as well as his wine and cheese. Having just settled a case involving the loss of the three smaller fingers on a client's left hand, caused by a malfunctioning chain on his John Deere, for a neat $17.5 million, he was, to say the least, not entirely poor. But he was frugal. Waste not, want not, he always said.

Weinstock's first wife had been an industrial designer who designed specialized machinery for producing wooden buttons; his second, more benignly, was a French chiropractor. Neither marriage, as they say, "worked out," less from bad intentions or malfeasance on either party's part than from the mutual incompatibility that naturally arises between any two human beings—particularly those of the opposite sex—over time. Both divorces were amiable, albeit expensive, and both marriages produced, as part of the natural equilibrium that tended to characterize Weinstock's life, two offspring, one of each gender.

He had also been an acceptable, albeit not prize-winning, father to his four children: Amos, Mary, Isaiah and Martha, each pair named as a compromise between his own Jewish past and the lapsed Catholic faiths of the women he tended to fall in love with. His first marriage was conducted by Rabbi Martin Siegel, the only such messenger of the Jewish faith that could be found willing to unite one of the Chosen People and a *goy* in holy matrimony. Rabbi Siegel had even written a best-selling book— so successful that it thrust him into the late-night company of

Dick Cavett—about the moral and spiritual agony involved in his decision to install an outdoor swimming pool behind his house in East Hampton.

At the ceremony, conducted at a friend's borrowed house in Sperryville, Virginia, a Catholic stood holding each of the four corners of the *huppah*, and—when Weinstock moved forward to crush the Biblical wine glass—he stepped, instead, on his first wife's foot, fracturing the large toe. Such, he feared, were the ways of men, particularly Jewish men.

Though he was now clearly on the downward slope of the bell-shaped curve, some things that were always true remained so: place, for example, a pair of tight jeans and some high-rising black boots on a woman, adorn her with some alluring undergarments from Victoria's Secret, and he could still rise to the occasion, senescence and erectile dysfunction be damned. The Bach Violin Concerto in D, whenever he heard it, still made him weep, as did "Listen to the Rhythm of the Falling Rain," and Frank Sinatra singing "New York, New York." In bagels, onion would always be his favorite; in sushi, yellowtail; when it came to the female anatomy, the ass, for whose elliptical and consoling flesh he could forgive a great deal that might be otherwise lacking in intellect and generosity of spirit.

Nonetheless, a friend's advice to the effect that what to look for in a woman, above all, was "emotional generosity," made more and more sense to him as the years went by . . . if only it had made more sense to his still-vivid sexual fantasies as well. The fact was that, if a good heart possessed even one tenth the erotic appeal of a nice ass, a good ninety percent of the world's great literature would never have been written, *Anna Karenina* and *Madame Bovary* included. And certainly no story, or novel, by a young person was ever going to tell you *that*.

Some years ago, while still married to the industrial designer, he had had a long drawn-out romance with a Hungarian woman, a curator at the State Opera. The first night they made love, on a mattress on the floor of the abandoned village priest's house Weinstock had just bought near Lake Balaton, he had asked her if she had ever before had a married man for a lover. In a curt, efficient couplet, she replied: "Only." Wisdom should surely have known then what it took lust another six years to discover, but wisdom, he had found, was slow on the uptake and long on regret. Wisdom, to say the least, was hardly a sexy word when something else had stood up in its seat, eager to get on with it.

The blessings of birds, they, too, were an acquired taste, and it was only in mid-life that the allures of the pileated woodpecker and the flightless grebe, and the sweet notes of the hermit thrush, had begun to soothe him. To have progressed from a fucker of women to a watcher of birds was no small matter, even for a man his age, and rising triglycerides and a swelling bladder might be only a further sign of the fact that wisdom was slowly planting its elusive nest in his sagging anatomy while mortality came quietly tiptoeing up to the door, preparing to knock.

It was during his marriage to his second wife, in fact, that the small glitches and anatomical idiosyncrasies that characterize mid-age began to manifest themselves, beginning with the random drippings of droppings from his slowly malfunctioning bladder, which his wife affectionately referred to, in her inimitable pidgen French, as *"gou-gouts."* Gou-gouts, for anyone who was interested, were the increasingly numerous (and, to a woman, apparently increasingly irritating) drops of urine that resisted even the vigorous post-urinary shaking of the male member and chose, instead, to deposit themselves on the un-uplifted toilet seat upon which the female *derrière* would soon reside. It was not, according to the French, the kind of thing that made for a good marriage, as were snoring and gazing at the passing *derrières* of younger women. *C'est la vie*, as the French said, and it seemed to be *la guerre* as well.

His middle years as an only mildly revivified single male had been memorable, as Shakespeare might have put it, more for the breach than the occasion, to say the least. The amorous life of a man who falls asleep every night at 9:30 and who rises between four and five times a night to pee—even if he has just settled a malpractice suit involving an operating room nurse who left her cell phone inside a patient's small intestine for a cool $8.6 million—was a much overrated experience, as was finding the kind of women he might be interested in on Match.com.

"Every man whose wife grows old has earned a younger woman," the Hungarian prime minister, Ferenc Gyurcsany indiscreetly had told the press when his own Socialist Party declined to keep his predecessor, Peter Medgyessy, in power. What he *hadn't* mentioned, however, was what a wife whose husband has grown old was entitled to. It seemed to Weinstock that she was entitled to quite a bit.

Nonetheless, the women seemed to be out there, in massive numbers, surfing away on the low tide of the net. One such forlorn lass, a dermatologist from Raleigh-Durham who described herself as "sixty-two, but with the body of a fourteen-year-old," had called him "the one man whose profile holds out any hope for an enduring long-term relationship," a compliment he was willing to live with for several weeks, until a group of her photos (her profile was marked "photo on request")—in each of which she looked something like a cross between Golda Meir and the Dalai Lama—arrived in his inbox, upon which Weinstock promptly checked the box marked "thank you very much for your interest, but I have just begun seeing someone new and would like to see how that relationship works out before meeting any new people."

Terribly civilized, the folks at Match.com seemed to be. And how cruel love, in mid-age, could be as well.

His chiropractor ex-wife, a health nut of all sorts, was wild for him to be in better shape, and—marriage being what it is—he had, of course, waited until the divorce was finalized to begin taking her advice. When he was not in court or on the phone with some hysterical plaintiff or opposing attorney, his hours were largely devoted to a combination of Pilates, bean sprouts, organic vegetables, homeopathic remedies, and books on Tantric sex, the latter of which were of even less interest in the increasingly abstract sexual universe in which he dwelt than they had been during his hey-day, in the '60s, when the twists and turns and slings and arrows of orgasm and its prolongation were, along with D.H. Lawrence's *Women in Love*, hot subjects among "sensitive" men.

"I know you don't know who I am, but I was once pregnant with your child, in 1971 or around there," a woman he knew back then, who had found him by googling all her ex-lovers, wrote just a few weeks ago, now some thirty-five years later. "I had an abortion at twelve weeks, but although I tried to dismiss it, I later came to feel deep regret because I was not able to have any more children, nor was I able to adopt any due to circumstances." Then came her recounting of the kind of history he had been hoping for: "Most of the other college seniors I knew seemed lacking in depth, unlike you. It's funny to think how if I ever started sharing with close girlfriends about his sex life I would always say, 'I once had sex with a guy in Binghamton who was very, very, very, very, very, very smart.' That's all I'd say because that's all I knew."

Yes, *very, very, very, very, very, very smart* . . . that was, apparently, what he once had been. And, from what his correspondent went on to relate, also rather sexy . . . albeit hardly overflowing with the milk of human kindness—not even the skimmed milk.

He *did* remember her, of course. He remembered her as having pale, somewhat freckled skin, as having studied as an exchange student in Germany (Freiburg, he recalled), as having lived right across the street from a former girlfriend of his, Deirdre McClintock, Olympic gold medalist of the blowjob, whom she claimed to have been able to watch from her kitchen window, fellating her married lover. He remembered her as he remembered them all . . . remembered them from what he used to refer as his "fuck 'em and dump 'em" days, days of wine and roses and woman-hating love.

"In the morning you were all businesslike, distant, cold," her letter went on, "and said you had to go and I could just lock the door behind me when I left. I didn't wonder, because I knew you were way out of his league, but it was after you left that I had the most fun. Here I had a whole house to myself, which I hadn't experienced for years! There was the beautiful fattish cat who seemed quite enamored of me even if you weren't, and a big kitchen which needed whipping into shape. I suddenly felt very domestic and decided to clean the kitchen—it needed a woman's touch badly. I whistled and hummed and tried to find different things to do to prolong his stay because I knew I'd never be back. I started fantasizing about being married and all that, which was totally new to me. Maybe it was the female hormones already kicking in. Reluctantly I let myself out."

Businesslike, distant, cold . . . that sounded about right. Sounded like someone he once knew, someone he once *was*. But that was another time, in that hormonal heyday when a man could still afford to be businesslike, distant, and cold. *Lang lang ist her,* as his father would have said. Long fucking ago.

Now, however, he was on the cusp of another, a kinder, gentler, epoch—what he called "the bad news days." Which was merely to say that a good seventy-five percent of the emails he got from friends were concerned with one or more of the following subjects: prostrate cancer, breast cancer, parental Alzheimer's, Parkinson's disease, suicide, adolescent depression, erectile dysfunction, and the search for tax-sheltered annuities.

"Just a quick note to let you know that my youngest brother Don died last Friday, from a massive heart attack," his friend Marsha had written last week. "He was fifty. The police came to our house to inform me. What a horror. Some people you can only miss when they are gone, and I miss him. Let us hope for more peace and love and hope in the new year, happy Hanukah."

What he himself was tyring to do now was to miss his friends and loved ones *before* they were gone, since he knew it was a one-way ticket and someone—either them or him—was going to get on the train first. Or, like his best friend John Wellberry, get run over by a drunk driver in London crossing the street when, like the good American he was, he was looking to his left.

In any case, it was certainly a far cry from fucking and blowjobs and good drugs and taking the LSATs. It was a far cry, too, from Dylan, The Cream, and Ultimate Spinach. And a long, long way from fuck 'em and leave 'em as well.

Speaking of blowjobs, his old girlfriend Deirdre—the first woman who had ever fellated him, on the carpet at 504 S. Liberty

Avenue in Endicott, New York, now some forty years ago, and who was now, as he was, on the cusp of sixty—kept threatening to reappear. "I will be heading north in his car on January 15," she had recently written from Asheville, North Carolina, where she now taught yoga. "It would be so nice to see you, share some time, catch up."

"Catch up" was, he believed, a euphemism in Deirdre's vernacular. What he wanted to explain to her, tactfully, was that there was no "catching up"—no, it was not their destiny to catch up, but, rather, to be caught up *with*. They hadn't, after all, "caught up" in over forty years, so, quite frankly, he couldn't imagine what her hurry was to do so now. What he suspected was that, if they "caught up," they would probably spend the rest of their unhurried lives wondering why they had ever been together (aside, that is, from that night on the carpet in Endicott) to begin with.

"I think it's very common for people to dig up people out of their past and try to reconnect," his friend David, a far wiser person than reluctantly ripening Deirdre, wrote to him recently, "with no other right to do so, really, than that the past once was. Our past selves have continued to exist in the fantasy life of others, which used to be innocent enough. But now such fantasies can become reality because we're all so reachable by everyone."

And so it was. The "past self" Deirdre was in search of was now an aging satyr with a leaky bladder and a severe subluxation between L-4 and L-5. The voluptuous, long-haired blonde with the magical lips was, no doubt, a cellulite-ravaged menopausal meditator who still read Ram Dass. But some among them, alas, didn't come around to the truth too easily.

The truth was that Weinstock was no longer at that stage of a man's life when a part of his anatomy woke up a full two hours before the rest. The force that once drove the green leaf through the flower now drove, for the most part, twenty miles under the speed limit, and on the right side of the road. Though Arlo Guthrie hadn't wanted a pickle, but merely to ride on his motorcycle, Weinstock himself, at this point in life, would decidedly have preferred the pickle, particularly if it was kosher. Such was the way of all things, and of all satyrs . . . provided, of course, they could keep their cholesterol down and avoid prostate cancer long enough to get there. In that sense, at least, he considered himself blessed.

The hall closet of the apartment he sometimes rented in Budapest—an apartment in which his friend's eighty-five-year-old mother had recently died—was filled with packages of still-unused diapers. Gazing at them each time he hung up his coat, he realized that he himself was probably now closer to his second "diaper era" than to his first. *Businesslike, distant, and cold* though he may once have been, he was now approaching the stage of life where those words would soon be replaced by *impotent, incontinent, and dull.* Like an old tiger no longer able to hunt on its own, he would soon be mooching off the carrion others had run down and captured. Such was the way of all flesh.

Recently he had gone with a Hungarian friend to a newly-released and very controversial film entitled *Taxidermia*, which included many scenes of various animals and humans being filleted, along with endless close-ups of animal and human viscera and interminable food-eating "contests" involving a variety of enormously fat men inhaling grotesque amounts of food and then vomiting profusely.

"It's a wonderful film," his friend had said as they left the theatre, "if you just don't look at it."

"Yes," he had answered. "Just like life."

But nonetheless, there were still days when what was risen rose again, when a young girl's eyes met his own on a train somewhere and he could have sworn he detected, on her part, a glimmer of what might at least have passed for curiosity; on his, for hope. As it happened, just the other day on the TGV between Paris and Marseille, when the young clarinetist sitting across from him, a beautiful young woman by the name of Romy with those classical French eyebrows and long, narrow ears like those of a deer, occasionally looked up at him half-flirtatiously from the pages of Victor Hugo's *Les Derniers Jours d'un Homme Condamné.*

Years ago, he would have gone to the ends of the earth for a girl like that; these days, he could hardly bring himself to go to the end of the bar. It was not so much that the possession would have been any less satisfying—perhaps even more so—but that the chase, the pursuit, all that frenzy and manic pouncing, had lost so much of their allure. Nonetheless, he couldn't resist smiling at her and looking back: Even if you can't go home again, you could still try and make the occasional visit.

Meanwhile, the bad news keeps pouring in. "To be honest," wrote his friend Marsha's husband, Jim, "things have been pretty awful. Marsha's parents are falling apart. Her father cries for hours about missing 'Don's hugs' and my mother-in-law berates him for not getting over it. They are both incredibly unkind toward Marsha, who is, needless to say, breaking her back to make things better for them. Don's son is trying to wrest away the next to worthless contents of his father's apartment from Marsha's other brother, John, who needs to sell whatever is left to help pay for Don's funeral. (Don had no money when he died, and was in debt to many people, including the IRS and yours truly.) In short, it's tragedy veering into madness. And by coincidence, my in-laws became officially insolvent last week. They have nothing left in their bank account. We are picking up the tab until Medicaid can kick in—probably two months at least. But this too shall pass, I tell myself. (What scares me, however, is what will suddenly appear to take its place.)"

Weinstock told his friend not to worry: what would appear to take its place would undoubtedly be better. But, deep inside, he wasn't so sure. They were, after all, God help them, on the downward slope of the bell shaped curve.

Good night and good luck, Edward R. Morrow, used to say to his television audience. And so, each night before he swallowed his Lipitor and his anti-coagulants, and placed the bedpan under the bed and went to sleep, he said it to himself as well. *Good night and good luck,* he whispered into the mirror, *good night and good luck.*

THE TRANSLATOR

It was largely because of my lifelong obsession with the mail that I began leaving notes for her in the artist colony mailroom.

"Liebes Fraülein," I began,

> Even the artist does not perpetually thrive in solitude. I have seen how you stare at me across the dining room table. Why not a romantic evening á deux? A quiet picnic on top of the mountain? A stroll among the ferns and wild flowers? If you will simply follow the fresh scent of men's cologne to my studio, or—better yet—leave a message in my mailbox, any of these might be arranged.

> A friend

As anticipated, her reply was not long coming. After breakfast, during the course of which—among more intellectual subjects—we discussed the caloric output required by lovemaking (I remembered reading somewhere between three thousand and four thousand. She, however, suggested that anyone with a healthy sensual life could hardly sustain such activity—"Are you sure it wasn't between three and four *hundred?*" she queried). I found the following note in my box:

> Counselor,
>
> Such flattery, such attention, must be high in calories! Alas—I am spoken for & feel most fervently in this attachment. I have, however, enjoyed our dinners together and hope this won't change.

I was disappointed, but undeterred. Waiting for her to disappear down the dirt road leading to her studio, I carefully printed the following note, which I ran to the kitchen and left in her lunch basket:

> Dear K.,
>
> Why such chagrin ("Alas") at the height of summer? I am, what's more, hard pressed to imagine a woman of your stature (and one, yet, who has been reading a book entitled *Women and Aggressiveness: The New Reality*) to be spoken "for." At best, I would think the preposition "with" might be more suitable, don't you?
>
> Why curtail one's vistas so precipitously? The wildflowers here have such lovely names: meadowsweet, loosestrife, bunchberry, heal-all. As my dear friend, Gerhardt, has so wisely observed—"One never regrets what one has done, only what one *hasn't* done."
>
> Why not reconsider? Our birth, as Wordsworth observed, is but a sleep and a forgetting . . . but our lives needn't be.
>
> Solicitously,
>
> H.

Thereupon followed, much to my dismay, days of silence. In the dining room—despite the fact that we were the only two vegetarians among the thirty-five colonists—she made a point of sitting as far from me as possible. As if this weren't enough, I noticed the next morning at breakfast that she was no longer reading *Women and Aggressiveness*, but rather a newly purchased copy of Simone de Beauvoir's *The Second Sex*. Though there was a heavy mist hanging over the New England hills, she wore a pair of dark blue sunglasses that prohibited even our usual eye contact.

Just as I was beginning to feel somewhat depressed, however (my work having come to a standstill, my mailbox having remained completely barren since her last note), I noticed a small, lavender envelope with my name rather elaborately calligraphed on it in green ink protruding form my small wooden cubicle. Hurriedly, I tore it open.

There, neatly printed in black ink on a sheet of deep yellow, fibrous rice paper, was the following message:

> H.,
>
> Have you ever heard of German poet Georg Heym? Perhaps you could tell me what the following lines mean in English:
>
> *Aber die Nächte werden*
> *Leerer num, Jahr um Jahr.*
> *Hier, wo dein Haupt lag, und leise*
> *Immer dein Atem war.*
>
> A brief note, of course, will suffice by way of reply.
>
> Merci,
> K.

My heart began to palpitate wildly, with unabashed jealousy, as I read these words. From whom else could she have received these words but from her "fervent attachment"? And, of all things, from Heym's most glorious love poem, *"Letzte Wache,"* which a poet of no less stature than Gottfried Benn had called one of the three greatest love poems of all time! And what now was *I* being asked to do, but to serve as the mere vehicle, the translator, of another man's passion?

Then, as if by divine interference, a thought struck me: Why not, by a subtle twist of the translator's precarious art, add my own dimension to Heym's lyric? Why not apply my gift, my own linguistic skill, in service to my own cause? It was, after all, *me* she had turned to as the Muse's intermediary, was it not? And what better test of her "fervent attachment" could there be than the one I now, in an epiphanous moment, thought of? Hadn't Shakespeare himself written it—"Love is not love / which alters when it alteration finds"? Excitedly, I ran to my studio to draft my reply:

> Dearest K.,
>
> How odd, that you should mention Heym, one of my very favorites . . . Do you know that he died (poor chap) in an ice-skating accident by drowning at the mere age of twenty-four? Such a brief, promising life snuffed out in the bud. The lines you refer to, happily, are among Heym's most beautiful, yet— typically—full of ambiguity and of Heym's insistent sense of the ephemeral nature of all love, an attitude which—rather obviously— you yourself don't share . . . not I.

They translate as follows:

Later the nights will follow
Richer by the year
Here where your head lay, and once,
Even your breathing was neat.

Hope this is helpful to you, its somewhat depressing message notwithstanding. The wild flowers, you'll notice, are now at the height of their brilliance.

Sympathetically,
H.

How clever of me! I thought. And how subtle. It was, after all, an equally beautiful lyric with "richer" substituted for "emptier" and "once" for "gentle," though, granted, slightly altered in meaning. However, I quickly reassured myself, Heym himself would scarcely have minded such a small alteration when its purpose was, ultimately, in the service of love.

That night, K. failed to appear at dinner, and I was informed by her friend Violette—upon voicing my concern as to her whereabouts—that she had gone to her room with "a slight headache . . . nothing serious."

"Yes," I remarked with appropriate empathy, "I haven't been feeling well today myself. Must be the pollen or something."

The next morning, much to my delight, K. was once again seated at the breakfast table, *sans* sunglasses and once again reading *Women and Aggressiveness*. I dashed quickly to my mailbox where, not unexpectedly, a white envelope, name scrawled hurriedly and almost illegibly across the front, protruded from the small cubbyhole with my name immaculately typed above it. I went directly to the men's room, where I tore the envelope open to find, in printed, ball-point handwriting that more closely resembled a child's than an adult's, the following message:

> H.,
>
> Are you *sure* about that translation?
>
> K.
>
> P.S. Did Heym ever marry??

The ball, clearly, had now been passed to my court. I needed to strike while the iron was still hot. I quickly scribbled:

> Dearest K.,
>
> Absolutely certain. German, you know, is my native language . . . better than English. Sorry, however, if the piece depresses you. It is, I agree, somewhat macabre.
>   Tonight, I might remind you, is the summer solstice, the longest day of the year. The sunset should be lovely from the mountaintop, don't you think?
>
> Ever fondly,
> H.
>
> P.S. Oh, I almost forgot—Heym, sadly, never married. It is suspected that—his adolescent tendencies toward romanticism notwithstanding—he harbored a deep disdain of all women. His mother, you know, was rather a severe manic-depressive.

It was, of course, no surprise to me to find K.'s usual seat at the dinner table vacant that evening, and again the next morning. "Seems she has a rather hearty touch of the flu," Violette reported dutifully.

"How unfortunate," I commiserated. "Such a shame, to be taken ill here of all places, where the undisturbed work time is so precious. *Do* tell her for me that if there's anything I can get for her, I'll be most glad to do so."

To reiterate the latter point, I went directly to my studio after breakfast and typed the following note, which I once again left in K.'s lunch basket:

> My dear K.,
>
> So sorry to hear you have been taken ill. If I might be so bold as to make a recommendation. I would suggest you discontinue reading Heym and try something, perhaps, a bit more uplifting—Rilke might do. Are you familiar, for example, with his famous "Liebeslied" (Lovesong) that begins: *"Wie soll ich meine Seele halten, dass / sie nicht an Deine rührt?"*
>
> I would, of course, gladly provide you with the translation, provided it interests you. Even more so, I would be most glad to come by your studio and read it to you personally. You would be surprised to find how uplifting and consoling the sweet trill of a gentle voice can be in times of illness or depression.
>
> Whoever introduced you to Heym, I might add, chose rather a dilute aphrodisiac for so lovely a time as this. Observers reported that the young man had a rather bitter expression—indeed, a scream—still frozen to his face when he was finally brought to the morgue.
>
> With best wishes for your speedy recovery.
> H.

Having satisfactorily dispatched my latest epistle and checked my mailbox (empty, as usual), I walked quietly back through the damp, mushroom-filled woods toward my studio, singing quietly to myself. The sun was just breaking through the clouds, and I felt intoxicated by what I sensed was my impending success with K., as already evidenced by the heightened level of our correspondence. At this very moment, I thought excitedly, my latest message was no doubt en route to her small brick studio at the other end of the colony's four hundred and fifty acre estate.

Between practicing my flute and working on my new poem, entitled "The Infidelity Sestina," the morning passed quickly, so much so that it seemed I had just sat down at my desk when the sound of the colony's green pickup truck bouncing down the dirt road toward my studio informed me that it must be close to noon. I heard the truck come to a halt and the screen door to my porch open and bang shut as the truck accelerated toward the more remote studios down the road. I opened the door and lifted the small wicker basket marked "Frost Studio" onto my work table, turning off the droning hum of the electric typewriter.

Opening the basket, I saw a yellow manila envelope protruding between the two wax paper bags of cheese slices and cucumber bits that constituted my diet lunch. My hands trembling, I tore open the envelope, on whose front the letter "H" had been weakly scrawled, and found the following message:

Dear H.,

So kind of you to be concerned about me. . . Might I ask a further brief favor of you? Perhaps you could translate the following stanza of poetry for me from the German:

Du bist wie eine Blume

So hold und schön und rein:
Ich schau dich an, und Wehmut
Schleicht mir ins Herz hinein.

I believe it's by a poet by the name of Heine,
isn't it?

With gratitude,
K.

P.S. I'd appreciate a quick reply . . . it's rather
important.

Crestfallen, I folded the note and returned it to the basket.
What stupidity! What sheer imperviousness and obstinacy! First
Heym and now, of all things, Heine! What pure sentimental drivel
and seduction! But rapidly my anger and jealousy give way to
renewed determination. What had worked once, I was sure, was
likely to succeed again. The bastard's insistence notwithstanding,
I would once again pour some few drops of my rather innocent
toxin into his ointment.

Aroused by my new resolve, I quickly rolled a fresh sheet
of twenty weight typing paper into my IBM Selectric and typed
out the following note:

My dearest K.,

Heine it is indeed. And, no doubt, from a
like source as that rather depressing Heym
lyric. Heine, of course, wrote some rather
lovely love poems, but this—alas [cleverly,
I thought to myself, I would use her own
term]—is hardly one of them. A translation
truest to the text—and sense—of the original
would go:

You are like a flower,

so delicate and short-lived:
When I look at you,
melancholy invades my heart.

As I suggested in my previous note, Rilke—
with whose work I am intimately familiar—
might well provide you with more comfort
and romance in this small bucolic village of
ours . . . Why such persistence, my dear, with
these morose pessimistic lyrics??

Your humble colleague,
H.

P.S. Heine, you know, was a Jew as well . . .
and, I believe, paralyzed when he wrote the
above.

Ah, what joy! How these mere, small nuances of language
could alter meaning. How—by merely substituting "short-lived"
for "pure" and "invades" for "steals into" I had once again, I hoped,
rescued my affair—and, more importantly, my correspondence—
from the dull embers of annihilation! Delighted and blissfully
self-satisfied, I sealed the envelope and, whistling an aria from
Il Forza del Destino, rushed toward the Main House, where—
making certain no one was watching me—I quietly deposited it
in K.'s otherwise empty mailbox.

Rather overjoyed with myself and with the deepening
promise of my and K.'s correspondence, I decided to take the
afternoon off and sit in the woods reading *The Magic Mountain*.
As fate has it during periods of self-created opportunity and
fruitfulness, I had just come upon one of Mann's many beautifully
rendered passages concerning time, one which seemed to aptly
characterize my own delicately balanced yet deeply gripping
predicament of the moment.

"Vacuity, monotony," Mann wrote, "have, indeed, the property of lingering out the moment and the hour and of making them tiresome . . . And, conversely, a full and interesting content can put wings to the hour and the day; yet it will lend to the general passage of time a weightiness, a breadth and solidity which cause the eventful years to flow far more slowly than those poor, bare, empty ones over which the wind passes and they are gone."

How startlingly true those words seemed! Inspired by sheer delight at my own inventiveness and by the perpetual intrigue of anticipating K.'s reply, the afternoon, quite literally, shot by, though it seemed to me—quite as Mann suggested—that the days since the inception of our correspondence had lingered and extended themselves so as to convey to me the sense that our intimacy had been seasoned and textured by years of acquaintance. How truly delightful, how rich, I thought to myself, as I heard the Main House dinner bell verify the fact that the afternoon had, amazingly, passed without my knowing it.

Briskly, I made my way beneath the overhanging pines and maples toward the dirt road that led to the dinner table and to my mailbox, where—this time, I was certain, and surely in a more decorous envelope—my next communication from K. would be waiting.

To my amazement, however, when I confidently reached toward the upper left hand corner of the three-tiered postbox where my cubicle lay, I saw only the dull, uninspired rectangle of empty space I so dreaded. Nervously, I shifted through the envelopes and cards in the adjacent boxes—Berman, Bilenski, Birkoff, and Cantor—certain that the missing response had inadvertently been misplaced in the afternoon sorting. But no—nothing.

My suspicions were now aroused. Doing my best to mask my state of severe agitation, I took my usual seat in the far corner of the dining room. Violette was already seated at the table, along with Rudolph, and beside him—where K. invariably sat—was, yes, an empty seat.

"Where's our fair friend today?" I asked with exaggerated casualness. "Still sick?"

"I'm not sure." Violette hesitated. "Haven't seen her all afternoon." A pause. "Or her car."

I gulped down my dinner—a watery, undercooked mushroom quiche—in complete silence, contemplating my next move and attempting to disguise my anxiously repeated glances toward the dining room door, through which—alas!—no one entered.

Had I, perhaps, been too precipitous, too indelicate? Why, after all, hadn't she even bothered to ask me for the translation of the Rilke lines? Perhaps, flustered, she had gone off to the local library and found a German-English dictionary?

Suddenly, the shadow of my own duplicity hung like a gray cloud over the evening. But no, I consoled myself on second thought, she had probably been so wounded by the brute's insensitivity, by my clever translations of Heym and Heine, that her anger and sense of betrayal had kept her from an immediate reply. By morning, after a good night's sleep, her anger and disappointment would surely transform themselves into feelings of tenderness for her true benefactor—myself. I needed only wait, be patient. Morning would surely bring a healthier prognosis . . . and a renewal of our correspondence.

That night, I slept fitfully, awakened by periodic nightmares. In one, I was drowning in a marshy, slime-infected pond while K. and a large, handsome man stood on the shore, pointing at me as they hugged and laughed hilariously. In another, I was ice-skating with K., who skated off the pond directly into another man's arms while I fell through the ice and drowned. In yet a third, the ghosts of Heym and Heine entered my room during the night and tied me to the bed with live cobras, reading me definitions while the snakes tightened their asphyxiating grasps around me. I awoke, terrified and exhausted, dressed rapidly and—without even brushing my teeth—headed for the Main House.

There, in my rather ominous looking mailbox, it was— not a letter, not a manila envelope, but merely a blank, twelve-cent postcard with my initials scrawled hurriedly on the address side. Expecting the worst, I slowly turned the card over to find the following terse message:

> H.,
>
> Have gone home. A family emergency.
>
> K.

Devastated, I crumpled the card in my hand, threw it to the floor, and rushed toward the back door, almost kicking Violette over on my way out.

"Oh," she stepped backwards. "It's you . . . You might like to know that K. left this morning. Some trouble at home, I believe . . . I think she mentioned having left something for you in your mailbox."

"Uhhh . . . yes, I know. Thank you . . .Yes, she did," I mumbled. "I . . . I'm terribly sorry to hear that."

"Yes, I'm sure you are." There was, it seemed to me, the faint trace of a smile beneath Violette's otherwise sullen expression. "I'm sure you are."

My mailbox sat completely empty for a full week. Despairingly, I plunged full force into my translations of Goethe and my critical article on the requited love poems of the medieval German lyric poet Walter von der Vogelweide. As Mann had so astutely observed, the hours seemed—despite my previous interest in my work—to drone on endlessly, while the days passed as if in a dreamlike trance.

On the morning of the eighth day after K.'s departure, I walked—as had, since her escape, become my habit—past the site of her former studio, taking a long detour through the woods on my way to breakfast. As per usual, I stopped first in the narrow passageway between the living and dining rooms where—with an increased sense of resignation—I checked my mail.

To my shocked and joyful amazement, there was, on this particular morning, a small pastel-colored envelope protruding ever so slightly from the box below my name. To my further surprise, I recognized K.'s originally firm yet delicate handwriting on the envelope. The dark, thick imprint of the lettering on the envelope, however, led me to believe it had been addressed in a somewhat less delicate mood than our previous correspondence.

Looking nervously around me, I snuck guiltily into the telephone booth beside the mailroom and tore the envelope, excitedly but cautiously, open. Inside, typewritten and totally bereft of the author's own handwriting, lay the following polemic:

> H.,
>
> You dirty bastard. What kind of a pervert are you anyway? In your perverse derangement—you will, I pray, squirm to discover—you have expedited the inevitable: I am getting married next Monday—to a *true* poet, not a deranged, psychopathic S.O. B. like yourself. Take the wildflowers and shove them up your desperate ass.

Hoping to never see you again,
K.

Without knowing it, I had bitten my lower lip so hard as I read the above that a small drop of blood fell from it directly onto K.'s typewritten salutation at the bottom. Wiping my mouth with the sleeve of my sweatshirt, I opened the phone booth door, took a book of matches from the mantel above the living room fireplace, and—with a furtive glance over my shoulders—lit a match to this final piece of K.'s correspondence and flung it into the dying embers of last night's still smoldering fire.

It took a full two weeks (during which time the only piece of mail I received was an overdue notice for *Crime and Punishment* from the Columbia University Library) to bring me out of my depression, helped along (finally) by a letter from my mother and a belated birthday card from my ex-wife (in which she enclosed a reminder about my overdue alimony payments).

K.'s cryptic dispatch, needless to say, was the last I heard from her, my own sincere—and, if I do say so myself, generous— apology ("Dear K. . . So terribly sorry. Translation, as you must realize, is a rather delicate art. My best wishes to you and your to-be. Faithfully, H.") and thoughtful, I thought, gift of Rilke's collected love poems (cloth bound) notwithstanding.

On the brighter side, however, the Colony granted me a two-week extension of my stay in order to complete work on the Goethe translations (I have decided to abandon the Vogelweide piece . . . too sentimental). This, gratefully, will allow me to remain into early September, when the fall foliage and smell of apples lend such a fragrant and euphoric tinge to the air and hints of romance blossom forth from the deep New England woods.

Also—and much to my delight—several new colonists have just arrived, among them a very delightful (and not unattractive) young painter from Cleveland, whom I shall call, for the present purposes, simply G. Her husband, I am told, is a wealthy industrialist some thirty years her senior who suffers from bouts of alcoholism and depression. He writes to her frequently, and even—or so she tells me—sends her assorted love poems from time to time. His favorite, interestingly enough, is Neruda, on whose work I did my master's thesis at Yale (entitled "Ambiguity and Deception in the Erotic Love Poems of Pablo Neruda").

The other morning, interestingly enough, G. asked me if I might—at my convenience, of course—have a few moments to spare to translate some of them for her, as her husband always sends them in the original Spanish, his theory being that it is the musicality—rather than the content—of the language that best conveys the meaning. I told her that—while, yes, I agreed with her husband as to the importance of Neruda's melodic diction—it was also the subtle nuances, the inherent ambiguities, of his language choices around which the poems often turned.

I told her, of course, that I would be most glad to help, though I was quite busy with my own work and had little time to get together personally. Perhaps, I suggested, she could simply leave the poems in my mailbox, which—rather conveniently—was directly above hers. I would, I assured her, work on them as quickly as possible. I would return them to her box as soon as I had finished. I would take great care, as always, with the translations.

THEY: AN ANTI-ROMANCE

1. He

He was trembling. He was trying to talk to her calmly—intimately without seeming intimate, seductively without seeming seductive. She was so much younger than he—young enough to be his daughter, old enough to be his lover. There were, after all, couples like them all over Paris, Prague, the Upper West Side.

From the moment she had walked into his office, he had been trembling. And now, as he very deliberately sat munching on his salad across from her in the semi-dark restaurant, he used his questions like surgical tools—prying, cleaving, exploring the dark interstices and openings.

He had been very unhappy, he realized, for some time now. He always realized it when, as now, he felt that some incipient happiness confronted him. How he hated his goodness! His forced virtue and sentimentality! How he hated his marriage, the constricted, habitual life it had lured him into! And now she was sitting across from him—not an escape exactly, but an ellipse . . . an ellipse back into the lost life of his passions and desires.

That she was beautiful there was no doubt—not beautiful inexactly, as a poet had once written. Beautiful exactly. Not in the cold, evasive, untouchable guise beauty so often insulated itself with, but in a way that was vulnerable, open, confused. As confused, perhaps, as he was confused.

"It seems to me these days that sexual energy drives most things," she wrote in the brief essay she submitted to get into his class, *"it adds an instant zesty flavor, like a shake of Accent, to an otherwise ordinary scene."* And now they were seated here, in this otherwise ordinary scene, the lower half of his body trembling so violently beneath the table that every morsel in his mouth seemed suddenly infused with that same zesty flavor.

"We might try, for example," he said, "to write about this lunch we're having . . . We might each try to write about what we thought the other was thinking."

She smiled.

"We might try writing it now," he went on, "right after we leave here. But we wouldn't have much distance from it. It would probably be muddled, confused, lacking in clarity."

"Yes," she said. "It probably would."

"Or we could try it tomorrow, after having slept on it. That might be better."

"Yes," she said. "That might be better."

Now it was tomorrow. He was no longer trembling, but he hadn't slept. He had gone home, after their lunch, and, placing a large pillow over the spot where his wife slept on their king-sized bed, scattered the seed of his desire and loneliness all over the pillow, exhausting his nervousness and his trembling. Then, for a few short minutes before going back to his office, he fell asleep.

2. She

She felt confused, uncertain. She liked the way he had smiled at her when she entered his office, liked the poem he had read about his grandfather that day at the first class meeting. He made her feel immediately comfortable, offering her the chair and sitting at her feet on his office porch beneath the orangish maple.

She was used to men finding her beautiful—younger men, older men, men she had thought of only as her friends. *"When I got to America,"* she wrote in her little essay, *"I taught my kindergarten class kissing games. The girls always chased the boys, pinned them down, and 'raped' them."*

She wondered if her little essay had excited him, given him the wrong idea. She was being serious, of course, and honest, because that was the point—wasn't it?—to be honest. And she didn't want, she really didn't want, to always be the victim of her beauty, she didn't want for beauty to become a wound, as a teacher had once told her it had been in the Irish folktale *Deirdre of the Sorrows*. She was glad to be beautiful, but she didn't want to be the archetypal tragic, beautiful mulatto. No, she didn't want to live *that* life.

Her father had been kind of a free-love type from the sixties, a Norwegian psychologist who met her mother while studying at Stanford. *"He believed kids should be aware,"* she had written in her essay. Now she wondered if he, too, seated across from her, had been a free-love type in the sixties. She wondered what he looked like naked, if his body was still young, what he might teach her. She wondered if her little essay had excited him.

"So sex, in a sense, is the meaning of life," her essay had ended. She wondered if that was right—was that all there is? She wondered if he—old enough to be her father, though he didn't look it—still thought so too? She wandered what happened to the meaning of life when you were married, when sex became a habit . . . or, possibly, disappeared.

3. He

He wondered what he should do with his desire. "The Difference Between Desire and Action in Jacques Lacan," was the title of a lecture he had just been invited to at the Center for Literary Studies. But what *was* the difference between desire and action? What ought it to be for him? Aside from squandering his seed all over his marital pillow, what should he *do* with his desire now?

"The truth will set you free," the old proverb went. But what truth, to his knowledge, had ever set *anyone* free? He was sick of proverbs anyway. Should he take her for a walk along the river, say to her: "Listen, I'm so helpless with desire for you, I don't know what to do about it"? Should he hope, as the advice-givers loved to write in the advice columns, that desire could be transmogrified to friendship? Should he content himself with the abstract wisdom that unfulfilled desire endured, whereas fulfilled desire expired and turned sour?

"I held out my hand for a shake, but found myself grabbing his ribcage and hugging him firmly," she wrote in the second piece she submitted, a short story. *"When I let him go, I got a good look at his face. He should have been my father, I thought."*

He could have been her father, he realized. *Then* he wouldn't have been sitting there, trembling, desiring her. But he already *was* a father. Thank God *he* hadn't had a daughter. But what if he were to wind up desiring his own son? (He had such beautiful little feet, his son, such soft skin.) He had had such a student once, a student whose father desired him . . . a student of his the year he'd taught at a mental institution in Upstate New York.

He imagined himself inside and out of her. He imagined his tongue, the taste of her, the scent. He imagined every possible circumnavigation of her body, everything he could teach her—or had she already been taught?

"I was the straightest, squarest member of my tenth grade class," she had written. *"I wore blazers and button-down shirts to school and was a member of the Junior Statesmen of America . . .*

"But I managed to get the largest, most smack-talking and womanizing jock on the football team as my first boyfriend. This was a dichotomy I loved: everyone wondered if we had 'done it,' but neither of us would tell."

He was wondering, too, if they had "done it." He was wondering *what* she had done, with whom, when, how. Did *anyone* ever get enough of love? Hadn't Yeats written: *"No man has ever lived that had enough / Of children's gratitude or woman's love"*? Wasn't he right? What possible happiness could yet one more add?

4. She

She knew she was still young, that anything could happen to her, that it would all be part of "experiencing" life. He, too, could be part of her experiencing life. "Live while you can," her father had urged her when she went to visit him in Oslo last spring, "or you'll only regret it later. Harvest experience."

He didn't look happy, she thought. He moved his face a bit too close to hers when they talked. He looked so hungry, starved in fact. But he was nice, smart, vaguely handsome. He had, she was sure, things to teach her. He *must* have things to teach her— about books, about life.

"I'm kind of glad you're not going to be in my class," he said to her when they first sat down. "It makes it easier to be friends."

But what did he mean by "friends?" What kind of friendship would a man his age—a man with a wife and child—want from her? What kind of friendship would *she* want from him?

5. He

"The sleek, expensive girls I teach," he remembered the poet's lines, "younger and pinker every year / Bloom gradually out of reach."

Had *she* bloomed out of reach?

"Teaching is just, plain and simple, a sexy thing to do," he offered, abandoning all subtlety. "When two people talk about what really matters to them, when two people open themselves up to what's intimate and personal and important—well, it's not all that easy to keep any one part of themselves entirely closed off."

"Uh hmm," she'd nodded. "Uh hmm."

6. She

She was thinking that there really wasn't much difference among people from between about twenty and fifty. They all seemed to be struggling with basically the same stuff: *love, career, love, career.* He looked young to her—no grey hair, such questing, personal eyes. Was he lost too? she wondered. Was he as confused as she was?

7. He

She seemed so calm, poised, so sure of herself. Was it beauty that had made her that way? Was it luck?

"The first rule of life," Oscar Wilde had written, "adopt a poise. . . . What the second is no one yet has discovered."

Why wasn't *he* better at adopting a poise? The self-confident professor? The secure intellectual? Why wasn't he better at being happy? At enjoying his wife and his family? At mourning his lost youth, his unlived life, and just getting on with it?

8. She

It was time to go get her measles vaccination. They had been sitting at lunch for almost two hours. "I don't usually like to eat lunch," he had said on their way to the restaurant, "it screws up the rest of my day."

He helped her on with her coat, lingering over her shoulder. He insisted on paying the check, though it made her a bit uncomfortable. "Next time," he said, making her feel both hopeful and frightened, "*you* can pay."

They walked out into the Square. It was raining. He nudged his umbrella gently rightwards so as to cover both their heads. "Thanks," she said, reaching out her hand as she began to turn in the opposite direction, "I had a really nice time."

9. He

He didn't quite know what he would do with the rest of his day. He was beginning to feel, as she turned to walk in the opposite direction, nervous—like a young boy at the end of an unrequited first date. He allowed the umbrella to linger a bit too far to the right of him, covering him with rain.

"Yes," he said, as her face began to turn away from his, "I had a nice time too." He turned to face the oncoming cars in the street. Rarely had he felt so confused, so restless, so entirely alone.

10. She

She found herself hardly thinking of him anymore a few days later. She had been to New York to see her boyfriend. They'd had

a wonderful time. *Yes,* he cried when he came inside her. *Yes, yes.*
Her boyfriend had such a beautiful body. They had had such fun,
dancing at various New York discotheques, drinking, listening to
Cole Porter, making love. "I want you to come to New York and
live with me after you graduate," he said the next morning over
breakfast. *Yes,* she said, *yes, I will.*

*What could she possibly have wanted with a man old
enough to be her father?—a man with a wife and child?* she
wondered. Her life, after all, was just beginning, and his—well,
his was off somewhere else, no doubt in some dark, ambiguous
mid-terrain.

She'd felt kind of sick—for days, in fact—after her
measles vaccination. But now she felt better. She'd always loved
the New England fall—the trees turning such glorious colors, the
leaves falling. It made her think of hot chocolate and sweaters,
of things that were warm and consoling. And now, with nothing
much else to do on a crisp, cold, late afternoon in October, she
thought she'd get herself some. She put on her fur hat and gloves.
What a perfect afternoon, she thought, for a cup of hot chocolate.

11. He

He'd looked into his wife's face, into her eyes, again last night
for the first time in a long while. She was beautiful, he realized
as though he had never seen her before—more beautiful, in fact,
than when they had first met . . . more weathered, more wizened,
more full of life. And his son—what a sweet, beautiful child!
What flesh and blood!

He'd been nervous for days after their lunch—nervous,
distracted, even depressed. "The ways we miss our life"—that

awful, terrifying line from the poet Randall Jarrell kept coming to him—"*are* life." For days he'd walked around daydreaming, lustful, restless, beleaguered. But now he was calm once again. His unhappiness, he realized, was only the unhappiness of life itself, the unhappiness of being contained in a single body.

He walked from his office toward Harvard Square. The leaves were fluttering, bright yellow and orange, from the maples all around him. *I'm going to die,* he thought to himself rather cheerfully. *One day, I'm going to die.* He loved these late autumn afternoons—the air crispening, the light slanting toward melancholy and darkness. They always made him want something warm and consoling inside him—like the warm milk and honey his mother had given him as a child, like hot cocoa. Why not, he thought, buy himself something warm to drink before going back home to his wife and son, back to the consoling warmth of his own home?

Whistling to himself, he passed a young woman in a fur hat, her hair braided to both sides in ponytails, her skin the color of warm cocoa. She was kind of pretty, he thought as they passed. She looked, he realized a short while later, vaguely familiar.

12. She

Dear M.,

You didn't seem to recognize me yesterday when we passed on the street (maybe it was because of the fur hat I was wearing)— or else you simply didn't want to talk—and I was feeling a bit too shy to intrude on what seemed to be your reveries. But I was wondering if we might get together again for lunch, or a drink, before I leave for the summer. (I'm going to New Orleans to live with my boyfriend, who just got a gig there playing jazz, before we move to New York.)

There are so few professors I feel I've had even the slightest chance to interact with on a more personal level during my four years here, and you seem like one of the few who's truly accessible to, and interested in, students. And I'm truly sorry I haven't had the time to be in touch again before this . . . it's been a busy year!

So, give me a call if you've got a free hour or so sometime soon. Or else I'll just surprise you and drop by your office, okay?

Looking forward to seeing you,
H.

13. He

Dear H.,

Thanks again so much for lunch. You didn't need to "treat," really, but I thoroughly enjoyed myself anyway.

Since you'll never be a student of mine (a fact about which, I must confess, I'm not sorry), and since the enclosed piece is a kind of "collaboration" between us—and since it was YOU who reminded me, so aptly, that "sexual energy drives most things"—I thought I would take the risk of sharing the enclosed little story I wrote last fall with you, my "co-author."

Hope you like—and aren't offended by—it. Being a person who came of age in the laidback '60s, I suppose, still allows me to do this sort of thing, my slightly graying hair notwithstanding!

See you again before you leave, huh?

Cheers,
M.

14. She

M.,

I find your story highly inappropriate to have sent me to read. Apparently you have severely misinterpreted my friendliness toward you last semester and over the past couple of weeks: in no way did I "come on" to you. Certainly you did not know me well enough to have sent me that story even if I had: I found it very intrusive and, in fact, consider it to be a form of sexual harassment, the kind you so ironically downplayed when we spoke last week. Since you seem not to understand why, I will outline the reasons for you for your future reference:

1. I came to you in a professional capacity, as a writing teacher, and although we discussed personal issues, and the short story I submitted to you dealt with personal issues, you should have responded to me in the vein in which I approached you.

2. The nature of the issues I wrote about last semester in no way gave you the right to exploit information about me that they revealed, and in fact should have made you all the more careful not to violate my confidence.

3. If you are so dedicated to cultivating open, friendly relations with members of the university community, particularly students, you must take care to maintain an environment of trust in the process. I feel you abused your position as a teacher in leading me to believe that you wished to advise me and help me as a writing student, and then pursuing other agendas of your own.

The letter you sent me disturbed me and will leave me, sadly, a lot more cautious in approaching other teachers for advice. I also do not want any more contact with you. I sincerely hope you do not act in the same way toward other female students in the future: though I am willing to let this matter drop and simply stop contact with you, such incidents with other women students could leave you very vulnerable professionally.

Yours,

H.

15. He

Dear H.,

It seems—sadly, for me at least—that you radically misinterpreted both my "story" and my reasons for sending it to you, which makes me feel both sad *and* sorry.

I sent you the story because, truly, I felt we were friends, and I trusted you to take it as it was written—as a work of imagination based, loosely, on two characters (you and I), but, in its emotional fantasies and internal workings, not at all equal, or reducible, to either. This, I must tell you—as I would as a teacher, as I will as a friend—is exactly what writers *must* do . . . and what actual people (professors, married men, students, etc.) certainly should NOT . . . or at least ought to do their damnedest to avoid.

I wrote this story because our lunch, along with your submission for my class, triggered a certain writerly (though, I must repeat, not ALL-that-autobiographical) fantasies in me— fantasies of what *might* occur between a certain not-so-old college writing professor and a certain not-so-young student, and of how such fantasies might evolve, seen from an interior perspective. This, believe it or not, is what I (and every writer I know) do in ALL my writing—we begin with actual characters, a few known events, and then allow whatever fantasies may come (fantasies I know to be at least partially "true" from my experience of myself and others) to "take over" those characters and give them an imaginary—repeat, IMAGINARY—life.

You, and anyone else who reads or writes, ought to realize: there is, thank God, a radical difference between what a person may be inspired to *write* (on paper) and what an actual human being ought, in his/her life, to *do*. In fact, one of the great ways in which literature has, traditionally, instructed us is NOT by being "politically correct," but by being, emphatically, politically incorrect—i.e. by showing us precisely how we ought *not* to live, and what are the costs of so living (see, for example, *Anna Karenina* or *Crime and Punishment*).

The *actual* me is, in fact a quite happily married, non-messing-around-with-students type of guy, who has a very clear sense of certain boundaries and their non-violation. The "actual" you, to be sure, in no way—or, at least, in no overt way—"came on" to me, as I (in real life) certainly know/knew. But—as a writer (repeat: as a *writer*) —the possibilities inherent in "our" story and our lunch were—well, how else can I say it?—rather *irresistible* to me, and (as is my writerly duty) I made of them, on paper, what I could.

Perhaps, stupidly, I trusted too much in your mature ability to make these kinds of distinctions, and—as I thought it, at best, unlikely that I would ever see you again—I felt there was no harm in sharing what I considered, happily, a kind of "collaboration" which I felt it would be unfair to undertake further without at least showing it to you. Even my "fictional" character, you must realize, has the good sense to know, at the end, that such fantasies are largely the product of a middle-aged mind afraid of death and groundedness. And his real-life creator, believe it or not, knows it as well.

So . . . how many *mea culpas* shall I utter here in order to satisfy you? I'm simply sorry that you took this, rather than as an act of trust, as an act of "harassment," and I have certainly learned from this that I need to be more cautious about *any* such relationships with students, imaginary or real. But you should know: what I've told you here is in no way any different than what I would stand by as a writer, teacher, advisor, mentor, friend, etc. in any other circumstance. I had—and *have*—no "other agendas" with you than trying to be friendly and helpful. If, in doing so, I may have stumbled across a story of my own, I can only, perhaps, regret, but not feel guilty for. In fact, were we not, now, about to go our separate ways into the *adult* world, I certainly would never even have shown you the story to begin with. But I assumed, wrongly, that you would take it for what it is: a work of fiction.

If you'd care to talk about this some more, I'd certainly be glad and eager to. If not, I can only say I'm sorry—and, I must confess, a tad surprised and hurt—to have had my intentions, and my very being, so radically misunderstood.

In any event, I wish you better than just well in New Orleans this summer, and in whatever you do in the future. Perhaps, someday soon, you'll be better able to see the truthfulness of what I've said here, and that literature—though it may sometimes be *better* than life—is certainly, thank God, not always equal to it.

Yours sincerely,
M.

16. She

She wondered if, indeed, he had been right—had she reacted too quickly, too emotionally? Had he really meant nothing more by showing her his "story" than to honor their friendship, to show his consideration of her as an equal? Maybe she shouldn't have shown the story to her friend Molly ("What a horny, disgusting sonuvabitch he is!" she had said on reading it) to begin with. Maybe she should merely have sat on her feelings, her perhaps childish reaction of anger and betrayal.

Now she felt a certain sadness enter her—a certain sadness for him as well as for herself—as she packed her bags to leave Cambridge, perhaps forever. It must be difficult, she suddenly thought to herself, being still fairly young and spending your time teaching bright, beautiful students, many of them on their way to a success and glory much greater than your own . . . young people who were blooming, as he had once put it, perpetually out of reach. It must be difficult to be married, to be tied down, settled, responsible . . . yet still hungry, still yearning.

She had liked his face, something about his openness and vulnerability, from the moment she'd first seen him. Maybe, even, she *had* felt a flicker of desire, of curiosity about what it would be like to be with a man his age, a man of his background and experience. She had, after all, been with older men before—men from whom she'd learned something, men whose attachment to her, even within the distorting revisions of memory, she still treasured and looked back upon fondly.

And she knew, of course—though she didn't like to exploit the fact—that she *was* beautiful (she'd been told too often, had studied her own face in the mirror too repeatedly, not to believe it). And she herself loved beauty—physical beauty, the beauty of beautiful words, the beauty of maples in early spring—as well as anyone else did.

Maybe she should write to him again, she thought to herself. Maybe she should stop by his office one more time before leaving. Life, after all, was so strange, so mixed, so incapable of any clear, unambiguous understanding. Wasn't that, after all, what college—what literature—had ultimately tried to teach her?

17. He

Packing his bags to take leave of Cambridge, perhaps forever, he felt badly. He *had*, of course, desired her—and who could blame him? She was, after all, beautiful . . . exactly.

But he had also behaved honorably, decently, He had never touched her, never made any overt suggestions, had done nothing to compromise his relationship with her as a potential teacher . . . even as a friend.

Yes, of course, he *had* "taken" parts of her letters, her conversation, and made them his own. He had used them in his so-called "story." But wasn't that, as he had tried to explain to her, what writers were *supposed* to do? Wasn't that what, all these years, he had been trying to teach his students? Wasn't this merely an example of that very tactful and considerate "theft" from actual life that a writer, in his or her work, had to insist on claiming the right to? (And wasn't it no less than T.S. Eliot himself who had said that "good poets borrow, great ones steal"?)

Life, he once again realized as he packed his books into boxes, was hopelessly complicated, hopelessly resistant to quick moralizing and easy answers. So why not, as a poet he admired once suggested, merely enjoy the freedom of knowing that scope eluded his grasp, that there was no finality of vision, that neither he nor anyone else was capable of perceiving anything completely?

An almost paralyzing sadness coursed through him as he sealed the last carton with masking tape and sat, possibly for the last time, watching the late light sift through the trees behind his office patio. Soon the days would grow shorter once more, just as his life, daily, was growing shorter as well. Soon, yet another time, he would have to begin again.

IL N'Y A PAS D'AMOUR HEUREUX

Bergmann believed with Freud that all happiness was sexual happiness, and it was with this in mind that, most mornings, he disembarked from the warmth of the bed he shared with his wife of ten years and ascended into the vineyards of the small Hungarian village of Hegymagas to visit his paramour in her small rented wine-making house on the hill.

His lover—a Hungarian painter in her late forties, whose smooth, deeply tanned skin and athletic build rendered her attractive in a manner one would usually have attributed to far younger women—rented the house each summer with her nine-year-old son, Marco, whose father, an Italian actor and opera singer, lived in Milan with his new young wife and their two small children.

Marco had not been the offspring of his mother's and the Italian's marriage, but, rather, of their long affair entered into when the actor was still married to his first wife, a Sri Lankan fashion designer, and terminated just as he was divorcing his third. On their very last night of lovemaking, the egg whose destiny it was to become Marco was impregnated with one of his father's peripatetic sperm, and Andrea Horvath was on her way to having at least part of that family she had always wished for, and, at the same time, dreaded.

Bergmann's lover, in fact, had never been married—she didn't believe in the institution and its various forms of enslavement—but had chosen instead to more or less live out her romantic life with a series of married men, of whom Bergmann was merely the latest incarnation. Perhaps she was, Bergmann suspected—and as an old girlfriend had once labeled *him*—"a lover of the *Verboten*."

This morning, just as Bergmann left his village house for his morning walk, his wife—a French girl from the *Midi* with whom Bergmann had already spent a decade—was listening to her favorite singer, George Brassens, on their cheap Hungarian-made stereo.

"Est-ce que tu comprends ces mots?" she'd asked just as he left the house.

"Il n'y a pas d'amour heureux," Brassens was singing in that dark, tragically sexy, voice of his. It was a sentiment Bergmann had, over the years, found himself more and more in agreement with, his inherently romantic sensibility notwithstanding—or, perhaps, as a result of it.

"Il n'y a pas d'amour heureux," he kept repeating as he headed up into the vineyards.

There might not be such a thing as happy love, he thought, but at least there *was* such a thing as happy lovemaking. Voltaire, or whoever it was, had it wrong: Not *every* animal was sad after sex. He, Bergmann, surely wasn't, and it was with hope in his heart and a tingling below the waist that he climbed the hill most mornings, awaiting those moments of reprieve from earthly pain that made men—especially married men in middle-age—long for romance, and women ravenous for love.

Il n'y a pas d'amour heureux. Such sad music, Bergmann thought, climbing the last hill that led to his lover's doorstep. *And yet, and yet . . .* One always hoped to be the exception to every possible rule, one hoped for rapture without misery, love without pain.

"I can be certain of only one thing," one of Bergmann's favorite French authors had written of her obsessive desire for her lover. "His desire or the absence of his desire. The one incontestable truth was visible merely by observing his cock." And who could argue with *that?*—that one certain indicator of passion which respected no borders, spoke only the language of desire, and knew no alienation from itself, no exile.

And what, Bergmann thought, could possibly be duller than the artificial insemination of desire by intention? *Je ne veux pas, donc je ne peux pas*, his organ seemed to say each time it was faced with the prospect of entering his wife's body. *I am not simply a moral animal.*

Bergmann sometimes felt that his whole life had been typified by the clash between his natural characteristics and the conditions of his life. His "natural characteristics" were, at this very moment, mounting the hill, while the conditions of his life— well, they remained down below. And what better way to describe Bergmann's life?—The satyr posing as the dutiful husband and father, the romantic disguised as a moralist.

"I tried, against every possible morality beyond desire, to stick my nose in every woman's crotch," might well be the words ultimately inscribed Bergmann's tombstone. Far more compelling than: *"Here lies Marcus Bergmann. He did his duty."*

"Often I had the impression of living that passion as if I had written a book," the French author had written. "And all that continuing up to the thought that it would be all the same to me to die after having arrived at the end of that passion—without ascribing a precise sense to 'the end of'—just as I would have been capable of dying after having finished writing this for several months."

To die after having arrived at the end of passion—to follow *le petit mort* directly with the big one, just as in that old joke about the death of Nelson Rockefeller: *he came and went at the same time.*

Bergmann's friend Richard, in a recent email from Berlin, seemed to be the only person who understood. "I often think there's a discrepancy between your devotion to Brigitte, to the family, of course to your son," Richard had written, "which is very evident when one is with all of you together, and a yearning for a kind of permanently unmarried state. At some point, all of this falls away and what remains, as someone I know wrote, is 'a pebble standing out in the grit / Going no place.'"

Bergmann didn't exactly relish the idea of "going no place." As he strode into the morning sunlight on the hill and into the beckoning vineyards, it was very much a sense of going *somewhere* that possessed him—a sense of entering into the beckoning arms, and the welcoming body, of his beloved.

Only two things in this life had ever seemed truly meaningful to him. The first was sexual love; the second—as Oscar Wilde might have put it—had yet to be identified. He loved flesh—his flesh, another's flesh, the music that emanated from the happy conjunctions of the two—and his wife's strong but sparsely endowed body had simply never quite seemed enough to satiate his earthly longings. It was the loss of self—in breast, buttock, thigh, anus—he was after, and, in order to lose that self, a certain amount of territory had to be explored.

Bergmann was also acutely aware of the fact that the village was a small and gossipy place, and that his early morning meanderings up the mountain had been noticed, at the very least, by Anikó, who ran the small ABC store he passed on his way. Bergmann's wife, too, had commented on his sudden increased interest in bird watching—a passion whose onset had coincided exactly with the arrival of his lover and her son for their annual summer vacation.

Bergmann and Andrea Horvath had met over a game of ping-pong in his neighbors', the Kántors', backyard the summer before, just before Bergmann's wife and son had arrived from France. "I've met the most wonderful woman here—a painter friend of the Kántors from Budapest," Bergmann, still unaware of the shifting contours of his own infatuation, naively informed Brigitte over the phone. "You'll love her."

Whether his wife would have really "loved" Andrea Horvath or not had already become irrelevant by the time she and their son arrived, when Bergmann's own feelings for the painter—released from their moorings by their first, passionate kiss in the shallow waters of Lake Balaton—had already been transmogrified from Platonic admiration to incipient love.

"The one paramount immediate happiness, the happiness of love," Bergmann recalled the lines from Proust, "softer, warmer upon the stone even than moss; robust, a ray of sunlight sufficing for it to spring into life and blossom into joy, even in the heart of winter."

It had not, of course, been the heart of winter when Bergmann's sun-soaked lips first met Andrea's, but, rather, the height of summer, and he—relaunched into his long-dormant poetic state by his lover's kiss and the feel of her scantily clad, warm, water-drenched flesh against his—had commemorated the moment of his erotic resuscitation in a verse composed in Berlin that previous spring:

We kissed for the first time in the water,
In the Balaton, in summer, not far from the shoreline
Where others were gathered, sleeping and sunning,
And no one suspecting love could blossom
On a mere boat of reeds, set in the water
At the Balaton, in Hungary, in what was last summer.

We then met, as lovers do, throughout the winter,
In the rain and the cold, far from the water,
In Vienna and Budapest, even in Nuremberg,
In hotel rooms and stations, in peaceful slumber.
Now the spring has arrived, with its birds and flowers,
And I sit in Berlin, filled with the same desire
For you, and for summer, and for that luscious water
In which fires were lit no mere cold can smother.

But *il n'y a pas d'amour heureux* . . . the words kept floating through his mind, even as arrived at his lover's cottage, where the painter sat contentedly on a white plastic chair, reading the collected works of the great Hungarian poet Endré Ady and gazing out toward the volcanic mountain of Szigliget.

"Oh, *Édesem*, I'm so happy to see you," she greeted Bergmann, using the Hungarian term of endearment that had become their own. "Would you like some coffee?"

It was Bergmann's and Andrea's good fortune both that

Marco was a late sleeper and that the cottage—which was none other than the one the Bergmanns themselves had rented for three consecutive summers before buying their own house in the village—came with an upstairs room, sparsely and conveniently furnished with several mattresses. Each morning, after coffee and some caresses in the vineyard-encircled yard, the lovers mounted the rose-trellised wooden stairs and entered the room, where—with virtue in their minds, and passion and transgression in their hearts—they sometimes roughly and half-violently, other times languorously and tenderly, made love.

"Do you know that song by Brassens?" Bergmann asked this particular morning, after an hour of lovemaking both so tender and so satisfying it brought tears of gratitude to his eyes. *Il n'y a pas d'amour heureux.*

"Yes," Andrea replied. "Of *course* I know it . . . *every* Hungarian knows it. Why, it could almost be our national anthem."

"And do you think it's true?" Bergmann responded with an almost childish innocence. "Is there no such thing as a happy love?"

"I'm not sure," his lover replied. "But what I do know is that we have just spent a *very* happy hour . . . a very, very happy hour."

"Yes." Bergmann sat up, gazing out over the balcony at the sun rising over Szigliget Mountain. "We have just spent a very happy hour."

On the cherry tree in front of the window, a small yellow warbler was singing. Overhead, the village stork, its beak filled with regurgitated Balaton carp, was heading back toward its nest. Bergmann was looking, now, further outward toward the Lake, the site of his and his lover's first kiss. As he watched her seeming to blossom out further and further from his reach, he thought again of that kiss, and of how, in another world than this, it might have been lit by fires no mere cold could smother, nor any simple song extinguish.

NETANYAHU'S MISTRESS

It was the contentious, unhappy era of Benjamin Netanyahu's first reign as Prime Minister of Israel, and I had arrived home from the Hebrew University in Jerusalem a bit early, having cancelled my second class of the day because of a bad cold. To my surprise, Prime Minister Netanyahu was seated at our kitchen table, having coffee with my wife.

"Bibi," I said, "what in the world are you doing here?" The Prime Minister looked just as I might have expected—like an overweight, out-of-shape boxer, a bit too beefy in the thighs, a life preserver's worth of paunch around the waist—in his underwear, a pair of green striped boxer shorts. A kind of Israeli Clinton, you might say, without the acne medication. The sort of man one would expect might have problems with interns and babysitters.

My wife, clearly a bit surprised to find me home so early, dropped two Saccharin tablets into Netanyahu's coffee, gazing up at me with a her classically *schiksa*-esque smile. On the kitchen table, a clutch of yellow roses in a blue ceramic vase I didn't recognize met my gaze.

"Would you like some coffee, *mon amour?*" my wife

asked solicitously. She knew I only drank Twining's Gunpowder Green Tea.

"Thanks," I said, with a wink. "Think I will."

Bibi looked pale, tired, a bit drawn as he sat at the table. "Tough week, eh?" I offered consolingly.

It *had* been a tough week for the Prime Minister: Nine Israeli girls shot dead by a crazed Jordanian officer near the border; daily stone-throwing in Hebron and East Jerusalem; almost weekly resolutions condemning Israel at the U.N.; Arafat holding a multi-nation "peace summit" (without Israel!) in Gaza. To make matters worse, a cognitive psychologist had just published a lengthy peace in *The Jerusalem Report* on "The Meaning of Body Language," which depicted the Prime Minister's wife, Sara, as the textbook example of the pathological liar. Who could blame the poor bastard for wanting a little something on the side?

My wife had just baked a *tarte aux pommes* and, with the air of a nurse sneaking a Godiva chocolate to a diabetic, cut a whopping slice for the Prime Minister, on which she placed a huge dollop of Dr. Lek's vanilla ice cream.

"Bibi's had a hard couple of days," she offered, turning to me like someone explaining an old uncle's infirmity to a long absent relative. "Severe pain in the fifth lumbar region."

My wife, a French chiropractor, had met the Prime Minister when he was referred to her for his recurrent back pain by a friend in Jerusalem—an American-Israeli journalist and second cousin of assassinated Rabbi Meier Kahane, who had known the Netanyahus during their time at the U.N., and who everyone was sure was a closet Likud *apparatchik*, if not worse.

"Arafat. Arafat. Arafat," the Prime Minister moaned, putting his head in his hands as he chewed on a widgeon of my wife's pure butter crust. "Everything that bastard does the world embraces, with his silly shawl and rotten teeth, while all I have to do is jiggle a bunch of stones in an abandoned field at Har Homar and they're ready to crucify me, pardon the bad pun."

I felt, despite the somewhat uncomfortable circumstances, a wave of pity for the beleaguered Prime Minister. Seated in his underwear at our kitchen table beside my wife, he resembled a vastly overgrown child, somewhat like Robin Williams in *Jack,* and, as I gazed at him, it seemed somehow difficult to grasp the media's repeated references to him as "handsome." But, then again, who was there to compare him to?—Shamir? Begin? Levi Eshkol? Golda Meir? Ben Gurion? The South Americans and Spaniards, after all, were the only ones allowed to have *truly* good-looking presidents, and we all know what *they* were worth when it came to deciding between their nations and their love lives.

The phone rang. I went to answer it. "I need to speak with the Prime Minister," a voice I recognized from television as belonging to the Prime Minister's top advisor, David Bar-Ilan, demanded. "Arafat's on the other line—it's urgent." At the same time, I heard the crisp crackle of what must have been a cellular phone, and suddenly a muffled, but unmistakable, voice broke it. "I must speak with Netanyahu, please," the voice demanded. Arafat himself.

As I turned to pass the phone to Netanyahu, who had just inhaled another bite of my wife's *tarte aux pommes* and was pulling his boxer shorts up over his navel, I couldn't help but think what my father, who had passed away just months before at the ripe old age of ninety-two, would have thought of all this were he, *hass bescholem,* still alive. Here was his son, seated at his kitchen table in Jerusalem with his *schiksa* wife and the Israeli Prime Minister, and none other than Yassar Arafat on the phone.

"Hello, Yassar? The Prime Minister grabbed the phone from my hands. "What's up?" Netanyahu, it couldn't be denied, had a way with words.

"Pull back the bulldozers? Are you crazy? I don't give a damn what Clinton said on CNN . . . or Madeline Albright, bless her grandmother, either. The bulldozers stay."

Arafat must have hung up, for, a second later, Netanyahu was back at the kitchen table, wiping a smear of cinnamon from his upper lick. "Fucking Arabs," he said, spitting a small dollop of apple into the air, "give them an inch, and they want the whole goddamned country."

My wife, apolitical to the core and reduced by my premature arrival to her professional role in the noble tradition of Clavdia Chauchat in *The Magic Mountain*, was studying the Prime Minister's x-rays, shaking her head sadly as she did so. "It looks to me," she said, pouring the Prime Minister another cup of coffee, "like a subluxation of the fifth lumbar."

"And the damned Americans," Netanyahu continued, ignoring this rather somber diagnosis, "think that—just because a couple of rich Jews from Saddle River and Scarsdale buy us a few museums and concert halls every few years—they own the whole country. Meanwhile, while they're safely at home *davening* in Great Neck and sending their kids to Princeton, our boys are dodging Arafat's stones in Hebron."

The Prime Minister's diatribe was interrupted once again by the ringing of the phone. "If it's Arafat again," Bibi called after me as I headed to answer it, "tell him I've just left."

The voice on the other end, however, was not Arafat's. It also sounded vaguely familiar.

"Is Dr. Leconte there please?" it said.

"And who may I say is calling?" I asked, somewhat

surprised by my wife's sudden, mid-afternoon, popularity.

"Shimon Peres," the voice answered. I had met Peres briefly once, at a Holocaust conference in Budapest, and, of course, had heard his voice countless times on radio and television. Sure enough, it sounded like the former Prime Minister on the other end. Like his successor, he too had been having a tough week— the kind, I suspected, which often resulted in back pain—as he seemed about to be evicted from the Labor Party leadership by a *sabra* named Ehud Barak.

"It's Peres," I called into the kitchen to my wife. "For you." I could see a not-so-subtle grimace, followed shortly by a tenuous smile, slide onto Bibi's face, almost obscuring the pimple just below the right corner of his mouth, as my wife headed for the phone.

"*Shalom,* Mr. Peres," I heard my wife say in her inimitable French accent, followed by a long pause.

"Well," she finally continued, "eet might be a bit awkward . . . you see, Prime Minister Netanyahu is here at the moment."

"It's no problem," I heard Bibi call out from the kitchen. "We're old friends." There had been rumors in recent weeks— hotly denied by both men—of secret meetings between Netanyahu and Peres aimed at forming a National Unity Government.

"I guess it's okay," I then heard my wife almost whisper into the phone. "He doesn't seem to mind. How about 2:30? Fine, see you then. *Shalom, shalom.*"

It was hardly twenty minutes later when, on our quiet, middle-class Jerusalem street near the German Colony speckled with white Subarus and BMWs, a black Lincoln Continental pulled up in front of our house, from which first a driver, and then Peres himself—his elegant gray-white hair gleaming in the sun— stepped out and entered through the opening in the stone wall that led to our door.

Peres and Netanyahu, in a scene, which somehow reminded me of an eagle embracing a pig, hugged warmly as the former Prime Minister entered.

"Nu, Shimon, was tut sich??" Netanyahu asked in Yiddish.

"Hass bescholem, Bibi, not much," Peres answered. "All I know is I wouldn't want your job for ten million shekels."

"You would have saved us *both* a lot of trouble, you *schnorrer,* if you had said that last year," Netanyahu joked, offering the former Prime Minister, obviously in pain, his seat.

My wife cut another slice of *tarte aux pommes*, on which, as if to emphasize the difference between the two men's anatomies, she placed not one, but *two*, huge scoops of Dr. Lek.

"Toda raba," the former Prime Minister smiled up at her, his smile quickly turning to a grimace as he changed position to sit down.

"Bevakasha," said my wife. "Just finish your pie, and—if the Prime Minister doesn't mind—you can go into my office and take off everything but your undershorts." Even my wife, whose tolerance for domestic drama was greatly enhanced by what I called her 'Frenchness,' was blushing now. "And lie face-down on the table."

"Lo, lo, I don't mind at all," Netanyahu, seeming distracted from his invective against Arafat, waved his hand generously into the air. "Poor Shimon"—and at this point I thought I saw him winking sneakily at my wife—"is obviously in worse pain than I am."

Peres—who, despite his present condition, was more youthful and better-looking than I remembered him—very deliberately, like a man preparing for a desert war, very deliberately bathed his remaining morsel of pie in the now-melted Dr. Lek, then slowly lifted himself from his chair, and, with the elegance of a wounded lion out of a Hemingway story, preceded by my wife, entered her treatment room, closing the door behind them.

I felt a bit awkward, sitting at my own kitchen table with the Israeli Prime Minister, a man all my friends detested, dressed only in his green boxer shorts, a smidgeon of apple skin dangling from the left side of his mouth.

"Your wife tells me you're a writer," the Prime Minister, obviously trying to break the uncomfortable silence between us, started in. "And a professor too . . . *Mazel tov.*"

"Why, thank you," I said politely, "though, of course, it's not much compared with being Prime Minister."

"Believe me," Netanyahu placed his chin in his palms on the kitchen table," it's not all it's cracked up to be. Just look at my life—the Arabs hate me, the secular Jews hate me, the Hassidim hate me, and the Americans hate me. Why, even Sara says in our pre-nuptial contract that she'll leave me if I don't win the next election. Which is why," he continued, growing rather apologetic, "I occasionally need a little something on the side. Believe me, you're better off lecturing on *Huckleberry Finn* at the Hebrew University."

Netanyahu seemed a pathetic, diminished figure as he sat before me, virtually caught *in corpus delecti* with my wife. And, as for *ma belle femme*—well, who could blame her? I was, after all, moody, impotent, angry, and dissatisfied, still tied to my dead and demented father's vision of my life as a good Jewish boy married to a veterinarian's daughter, living out my adult years in a duplex beside him and my stepmother in Jackson Heights.

"I'm not so sure about that," I countered half-heartedly, "but at least I don't have to keep going to parties with people who hate me." I had just watched, the other night on television, as the Prime Minister stood, like Hamlet beside Gertrude, next to Leah Rabin—whose eyes, had they been daggers, would not merely have beheaded, but also castrated, him—at a dedication ceremony for a new children's center in Tel Aviv.

Netanyahu seemed on the verge of tears as he spoke, but was saved from any further embarrassment by the ringing of our telephone, which I answered to discover a raspy, rather otherworldly, voice on the other end.

"Is Dr. Leconte there, *bevakasha?*" it asked.

"I'm afraid she's with a patient. May I take a message?"

"It's rather urgent. Yitzhak Rabin here. I have a very bad back."

"Yitzhak Rabin! Aw gimme a break, will you?" I said, sounding suddenly very American, "You've been dead for more than a year. Remember Yigal Amir?"

"Stupid boy," the voice, which suddenly reminded me of Bernard Malamud's, admonished me. "Don't you know a Jew *never* dies, especially at the hands of an assassin? Didn't they teach you anything in Hebrew School? Aren't you ashamed of yourself?"

"Well, listen, Mr. Prime Minister," I said, looking over at Netanyahu, who seemed utterly unperturbed by our conversation, "if you're so alive and all that, why don't you just leave me your telephone number, and I'll have my wife give you a call just as soon as she's done with Shimon Peres, okay?"

"Ach Gott, *he's* got back trouble too?" the voice asked, a tone of commiseration creeping in. "Give him my love. I'll call back later." With that, the line went dead.

Netanyahu looked up from the kitchen table, observing what must have been the whitened expression on my face. "Not to worry," he said, finally wiping the smidgeon of apple from his mouth, "he calls me all the time. Those old Jewish soldiers never die, they only fade away."

By this time, Peres, smiling now and followed by my wife, who seemed to be re-arranging herself from a state of relative disarray, entered from the treatment room and rejoined us at the kitchen table.

"Who was that on the phone?" my wife asked, refilling our coffee cups.

"Oh, no one special—just Yitzhak Rabin."

"Him again?" she bristled. "Those dead guys have more back problems . . . "

"Well," said Peres suddenly, looking at his watch, "I really better get going. We have a Labor Party meeting tonight in Jerusalem—another no-confidence vote against the government, you know." Netanyahu groaned, digging his face into his palms. Just then, the phone rang again. I went to pick it up.

"Michael, *mein Sohn*" I heard my father's voice on the other end. "I'm so proud—so *schtoltz*—of you, *hass bescholem*."

"Dad!" I screamed into the receiver. "What the hell are *you* doing on the phone? You're dead too, for Christ's sake!"

"Christ? For this I brought you up for forty years like a good Jew?"

"Sorry, dad, I meant Moses."

"Don't you know," my father's voice, sounding healthier and livelier than it had in years, continued "a Jewish father is *never* dead. I'm here with Rabin. And I can't tell you how much it means to me to see you there with all those Jews—*soll sein gebenscht*. I always *knew* you were going to come—how do they say in English?—'around' some day, dear son."

Both Peres and Netanyahu seemed suddenly in a hurry to leave. The Prime Minister frantically tucked in his shirt, zipped the fly of his dark blue trousers, and tied his shoelaces as they stumbled, together, out the door. I noticed, as he turned, a large blue hickey on the left side of his neck. My wife blew Peres a kiss and handed him a tightly folded note as the former Prime Minister left.

"Dad," I said, turning back to the receiver, "what the hell are you talking about? What are you doing calling me up again? You're fucking dead! I was at your funeral! My son and I threw dirt on your coffin! I said *Kaddish* for you at your old synagogue! You disinherited me! I cursed your spirit! Why can't you finally *leave me alone?*"

"Aren't you ashamed of yourself, to talk this way to your old, sick father?" The voice and the cadence, now—not to mention the message—were unmistakably his. "An *alter Yid* is *never* dead, don't you know that? Especially when he is your father."

I was beginning to feel sick, a reverse peristaltic tremor invading my entire body. I felt an acute pain in what my wife undoubtedly would have concluded was the fifth lumbar region.

My wife smiled at me from the doorway. "Hang up on the bastard and have another slice of *tarte aux pommes*," she stroked my sleeve and whispered in my ear. "You'll feel better in no time, believe me."

VAJDA'S RESURRECTION

Bergmann received word of Vajda's death, not from Budapest directly, but by way of a phone call from his friends Milka and her Hungarian husband, Kalman, in Tel Aviv.

"We have some bad news from Budapest, I must tell you," Milka announced in a subdued voice. Bergmann thought immediately of his friend, the novelist K., who had recently suffered what he described as *"eine kleine Herz infraktion"* in Berlin, requiring a triple bypass, or of his old friend, Magda Weinstock, 92, whose heart wasn't in all that great shape either. Or of Benedek Varkonyi's mother, bedridden with ovarian cancer. Or of the poet Földényi. Or the architect Bor.

"András Vajda died two weeks ago of cancer," Milka continued. "Someone called Kalman at his Budapest studio to tell him. . . . We were both completely shocked. Such a *tzores*."

Bergmann felt a deep chill run down his spine at the thought of Vajda—Vajda, whom he had just seen, resplendent in his new imported leather jacket and black jeans at his just-finished house along the Danube in August; Vajda the TV star; Vajda *pater familias* of a second family and new baby girl, father to a small harem of four women (six, if you included his present and former

185

wives); Vajda the exerciser, swimmer, indulger in Budapestian mineral waters; Vajda the world traveler, the *bon vivant*, the good time boy . . . Vajda, exactly the same age, almost to the day, as Bergmann himself.

"You won't believe it," Bergmann greeted his wife, just back from the gardening center. "Vajda's dead."

"Vajda?" Bergmann's wife dropped a large bag of vulture manure at her feet. "Impossible. He's the same age as you are, isn't he?"

"He's not now," Bergmann quipped somberly. "Cancer of *la rate,* Milka says . . . she didn't know the word in English."

"The spleen," Bergmann's wife provided. "It's a killer."

"It sure is," Bergmann agreed.

All afternoon, images of Vajda—Vajda the neighbor, Vajda the journalist, Vajda the proud father, Vajda the man about town, Vajda the not-so-young hunk—floated through Bergmann's mind as he wrote, gardened, ate, thought about sex and the body's circumscribed and circumscribable pleasures.

My dear András, he finally sat down at his computer and composed an email to another Hungarian András, this one the architect Bor, who had designed the Vajdas' just-completed house:

> We were shocked, just a half hour ago, to receive a call from Milka and Kalman in Tel Aviv telling us that Vajda had died. How absolutely awful, and unjust! We are utterly speechless, and all I can say is that it is a warning to the rest of us to treasure—and relish—every single day, every sunset and sunrise. How terrible for Zsuzsa and the girls. What a strange and cruel God lives up there.
>
> Please convey to Nóra, if you see her, our heartfelt sympathy and shock. We will write to them soon.

And, of course, our fondest greetings to you all.

—Bergmann

There was, of course, within Bergmann—along with his genuine grief, and sense of loss at having someone so young, in the prime of life and at the apex of his achievements, snatched form this earth—that certain sense of elation that always accompanies tragedies befalling others: It had, after all, not happened to *him*. He, Bergmann, was still alive and kicking, with his fresh piles of vulture manure and compost, his newly planted trumpet vines and hydrangeas, his still unlived infidelities and betrayals. Like the grandmother to whom he had once read the weekly obituaries in New York's German-Jewish *Aufbau,* he was a survivor: Vajda was gone; Bergmann was still here.

All afternoon, poems and epistolary expressions of sympathy poured from him as he worked and pondered. *"Kedves Nóra,"* he began mentally, *"We are in a state of utter shock and disbelief at the news, just received from Milka and Kalman, of András's sudden and tragic death . . . What a terrible, terrible loss for you and the girls."*

"I keep seeing him standing right here in front of me," Bergmann said to his wife, who was planting a honeysuckle vine and some purple sage, "just last August, in his leather jacket, in front of that beautiful new house of theirs . . . The guy just had *everything* going for him—looks, money, success, family, health, optimism. And, now—whammo!!"

"Oui, chèrie," Bergmann's wife, a country girl from Provence, countered, "eet is why I am always telling you to treasure what we have. *La vie est courte* . . . Sometimes more *courte* than we think."

"Yes," countered Bergmann it can be *courte* indeed."

***

After receiving the news of Vajda's premature demise, and before his wife had returned from the gardening center, Bergmann went downstairs to their bedroom, covered their stuffed green bolster with an old gym towel, and shot a not-insubstantial wad of his living seed onto the towel, as if to reassure himself that *he*, at least, was still among the living.

Sex was something Bergmann and his wife no longer had much of—it had, in fact, been years since their last, abortive attempt at lovemaking—and, for Bergmann at least, the thought of Vajda's just-born youngest child was not unlike a stone placed on Oscar Schindler's grave at Yad Vashem. Vajda, at least, had left a mini-armada of progeny and ex-wives in the world to fuel the living candle of his flame.

For Bergmann, however, with merely his one accidental child and one, long forgotten, ex-wife, immortality seemed a more tenuous prospect. (Not to mention that, unlike Vajda, there was no mini-archive of Bergmann memorabilia in the world's stored journalistic repositories; rather, only a small handful of remaindered books read largely by intimates and past intimates yearning to recognize themselves among the thinly disguised characters.) If Vajda was dead, he asked himself as the small puddle of microscopic tadpoles slithered out onto his abused gym towel, could he, Bergmann, be very far behind?

Life, he realized, was certainly a fickle affair. At his very moment, in fact, Bergmann's 92-year-old stepmother, suffering from cancer, osteoporosis, a broken hip, several cracked ribs, a punctured lung, diabetes, and countless other maladies, was in her sixth month on a respirator, while poor Vajda, the epitome of robust health and good cheer, was—in the company of his more famous Hungarian compatriots Imre Nagy, János Kadar and György Lukács—being devoured by worms beneath the Hungarian earth. What justice was there to all this? Bergmann pondered. Or what sense?

***

Vajda's eldest daughter, Zsuzsa, a high school senior at the time, had been the Bergmanns' first babysitter in Budapest several years ago. A dark-haired, vixen-like creature with deep brown eyes, she was known, among other things, for generously fellating, à la Monica Lewinsky, a large harem of mostly expatriate American young men in various Budapest late-night discotheques and bars, the pleasures of which she had not been above recounting to Bergmann on various week-end nights when he drove her to the metro station near his house after her more domestic evening *chez lui*. Bergmann had run into her—recently married, and now working as a dispenser of, and proselytizer for, Shiatsu massage (still, Bergmann couldn't help noticing, passionately interested in the body)—at an outdoor café on Andrássy út just days before last seeing her now-departed father.

Going downstairs to whack off after hearing the news of Vajda's premature demise, it had been, Bergmann now realized, young Zsuzsa's fellatio-ridden face, rather than his wife's more domesticated features, that had risen from the smoky curlicues of his fantasies, and now he thought of her, and of her slightly younger sister, Dóra, a devout member of Budapest's growing Scientology community, whose proclivity for having rings and pearls inserted through various parts of her anatomy (nostrils, tongue, belly button . . . only God knew where else) had long ago eliminated her from the wide-roving range of Bergmann's erotic fantasies.

Later that afternoon, haunted by images of still-breathing, leather-jacketed, younger-looking and handsomer-than-he-was Vajda, Bergmann left his wife to her potpourri of one third vulture manure, one third compost and one third Texas soil, and went inside to log onto his email once again. In a state of astonishment bordering on disbelief, the screen now uttered forth the following words:

Dear Friends,

First of all, Vajda András is alive!

A stupid news has spread in newspapers and radio without checking if true. Imagine the whole country is wired up, imagine how many calls and reporters. He does not want to do anything against it because it would be even worst. He thinks about celebrating his own funeral, but he feels no like. So do not write her, except something happier. I let this know Kalman and Milka too. Is not it fantastic the information? First a fake, than goes from Hungary to Israel, than to Texas, than to Budapest maybe in a day.

Hug to you all—
András

"Chèrie, you won't believe it!" Bergmann ran out into the garden, waving the emailed message into the languid Texas air.

"Won't believe what?"

"Vajda has been resurrected."

Bergmann's wife looked up from the strawberry patch, her not infrequent I-married-a-crazy look coming over her face. "What in the world are you talking about? Resurrected? *Est-ce que tu es folle?"*

"You don't believe me?" Bergmann shoved the piece of paper under his wife's nose. "Here . . . check it out."

"Amazing." Bergmann's wife was suddenly rendered speechless. "Completely beyond belief."

And so it was—beyond belief. Vajda, gone forever just hours earlier, was now alive once again, perhaps—at this very moment—sending a shot glass of his semen into his grateful wife in search of the egg that would ultimately hatch into daughter #5.

Promptly the next morning, Bergmann sat down at his computer and sent the following message to their friendly architect, Bor:

Kedves baratom:

Now that Vajda is alive again, another question— Was Vajda really sick?? Was the whole business a "phony"?? How did this strange story come about?? You Hungarians are such fabulous inventors of tales!! Please let us know . . . tout le monde est curieux!

Bergmann

***

Vajda, as has already been mentioned, was a rather attractive man, very much in the public eye of Budapest's journalistic and social life. As was the habit with such men, particularly in Budapest, there had always been a bevy of eager women circling the periphery, like vultures, for the almost inevitable romantic decline, a phenomenon that led to marriage after marriage turning into road kill along the highways of love and disillusion.

Though Vajda's marriage to Nóra had been, relatively speaking, a good one, there were those—such as a certain fellow

Hungarian journalist by the name of Lilli Rakovszka—who lacked the patience to wait out the inevitable Hungarian *dénouement*. This very Lilli, hardly a rose by any other name and amid the frustration of finding her attentions unreciprocated, came upon the idea of calling a local radio station to inform them that—although the family wished to keep the news momentarily private—András Vajda had moved on to the non-journalistic netherworld.

Rakovszka, herself something of a *femme fatale* in her younger days, still longed for the *Sturm und Drang* of romance. She had first focused her gaze on Vajda years before, when she accompanied him as a production assistant to interview the Dalai Lama in Tibet. There, over *nasi goreng* and various other Asian delicacies consumed in the high Himalayas, they had indulged in the type of more or less innocent flirtation Vajda was hardly immune to during his travels with often younger, and highly available, women.

But Vajda had sensed something rather dangerous about the hardly unalluring Rakovszka and had, for once, kept his fly zipped and his hands in his pockets. Upon their return to Budapest, Rakovszka had made her presence anything but scarce in the vicinity of his editing studio, repeatedly calling him to suggest a luncheon meeting or a drink to discuss, as she put it, "future joint projects"—offers that Vajda, sensing danger, had always politely refused.

But Rakovszka was not a woman to be easily discouraged, and, when rumors began circulating to the effect that Vajda's marriage had become more of a friendly cohabitation than a love affair, it occurred to her that the time might be ripe for some benign intercession on her part. It was just then, propinquitously, that the news of Vajda's illness and hospitalization became public knowledge, and Rakovszka knew all too well (she had been married three times, always to rather famous men) what a lethal effect the combination of illness and public attention could have on an already fragile union.

And so it was that, on the morning of Vajda's surgery for—of all things—testicular cancer, Rakovszka walked down to the corner of her *Rozsadom* flat in the Buda hills and placed a call from a telephone booth to the news desk of Magyar Radio, informing them that the living icon of Hungarian television, András Vajda, was no more.

Needless to say, in Budapest, where rumors of even an innocent tryst tended to spread like wildfire, the news of Vajda's passing was front-page fodder, aided and abetted by a close network of friends and "groupies." Within a half hour of Rakovszka's call to the radio station, the phone had rung in Nóra and András Vajda's newly renovated Óbuda mansion, with a sympathetic voice on the other end offering the grieving widow a once-in-a-deathtime discount on a high-end funeral at Kerepesi Cemetery, complete with limousine service to and from the cemetery and lifetime gravesite care—all for a mere 350,000 forints, VAT included.

Vajda, however—as luck and the best Hungarian doctors money could buy would have it—recovered. Within months— having temporarily suspended both his programs, and with the news of his resurrection having now surfaced—he once more became a ubiquitous presence on Hungarian airwaves and television sets, openly discussing both his narrow brush with death, and his avowed wish to "spend more time with my family," a wish which—along with others less morally wholesome, and more erotically diverse—had been pronounced by the lips of many a dying man in the past.

Why, even Bergmann himself could commiserate with such noble intentions.

***

Several months later, while the Bergmanns were vacationing at their summer home in Hegymagas, a piece of rather shocking—though in retrospect also rather predictable—news again appeared on Bergmann's computer screen:

"Dear David," began the message, once again from the Bergmanns' friend Milka in Tel Aviv, to whom even Hungarian gossip quickly made its way, "have you heard the shocking news about the Vajdas?"

Bergmann scanned the to-him-surprising, but not entirely shocking, news: András Vajda, it seemed, had taken up with a twenty-six-year-old production assistant—younger than both his older daughters—from his former office, while Nóra, at around the same time, had gotten involved with the carpenter who built the bookshelves for their new house, the latter who was apparently divorcing his wife.

What's more—and this was the *truly* Hungarian part—the newly re-aligned foursome had apparently become fast friends, enjoying cozy evenings together over bridge and Hungarian Scrabble. András and Nóra, the message continued, were selling their new house and buying another apartment on Vizsegradi út, halfway between their old one (where Nóra would live with the children and her new lover) and the apartment of András's young girlfriend, who still lived with her mother.

Bergmann took a deep breath as he read, and smiled. It was summer. There were birds chirping in the yard. Vajda was alive. The earth was a place of change and transformation, of desires untamable even by death. It was, he told himself, a good place to inhabit, despite all its suffering, and all its many changes.

***

Vajda's wife, Nóra, a woman with a now-prolonged history of getting involved with famous—and therefore, of course, rather egocentric—men, had, for some time before her husband's illness, been wanting a second child. Having recently turned forty, she had been listening to the not-so-subtle ticking of her biological clock, and the beat she heard was most frequently a rather monotone: *now.*

Vajda, on the other hand, already had two grown daughters from his previous marriage, as well as a third daughter, Eszter, now eight, with Nóra, and had long ago decided that his quota of progeny had been filled. Yet Nóra's insistence that her biological clock and the spacious confines of their new abode cried out for another little body—accompanied by her increasingly foul humor and attempts to sabotage the couple's usual method of birth control (the pill)—had finally met, some two years previous to Vajda's illness, with success: Hardly a month after moving into their new Óbuda house, Nóra's morning pregnancy test boldly announced that, thanks to their rather unenthusiastic lovemaking of a few nights earlier, yet another future Vajda was now blossoming, cell by dividing cell, in her body.

Vajda, to say the least, was hardly enthused at the prospect of having his *pater familias* extended further, so that when, just four months later, the hardly half-formed little girl was ejected from her mother, stillborn, in a whirlpool of blood, it took but very little time for Nóra Vajda to blame her husband's ill will and ambivalence for the premature demise of what would have been her second child.

Faced with the increasing *animus* and estrangement of his wife, there was little else András Vajda could do: He would have to try again. Within six weeks of her miscarriage, Nóra Vajda's underbelly was once again home to a rapidly expanding fetus—one, this time, she was utterly determined to keep until its natural entry into the world of the living. Nine months later to the day, András and Nóra Vajda's second daughter, Judit, came wailing into the world.

For the salvation of the Vajdas' marriage, however, the little girl's arrival came too late. Unable to muster even a scintilla of enthusiasm for his new daughter, and with his wife's anger at him over his prolonged refusals and ambivalence having turned a corner from which it could no longer glide into reverse, András Vajda—just a few short weeks before the acute pain in his testicular region led to a first visit to the internist—moved his belongings into the downstairs guestroom, and the Vajdas' conjugal relations came to an icy, and rather premature, end.

The carpenter who was doing the renovation work in András's new study, as it turned out—a well-built and vigorous seeming man by the name of Mihály Konrád—was just the sort of fellow to whom Nóra Vajda, in her newly maternal and maritally estranged condition, was most vulnerable. Within a week of her husband's being admitted to the hospital for surgery, a certain feminine vengefulness coupled with the carpenter's reciprocating ardor led the two of them, rather gleefully, into Vajda's just-vacated guestroom bed, where they proceeded to spend a large portion of András Vajda's post-surgical recovery. By the time András, a bit less of a man than he had been on his departure, returned home, the marriage was, more or less, over, and he could retreat into the conveniently self-pitying, and self-righteous, role of the betrayed husband whose deceiving wife had lured a young carpenter into her bed while he lay near death

Vajda, in fact, as we already know, did not die. And, once the news of the impending dissolution of his marriage became public, he quickly—in a series of well-publicized, and widely disseminated, interviews—changed his tune from that of the well-meaning and repentant family man to that of the grievously wronged, and mercilessly cuckolded, husband.

Ah, the ingratitude of famous men's wives! the good citizens of Budapest muttered in dismay.

Vajda, however, though wounded, was hardly down for the count: Within a few days of putting their new Obuda mansion up for sale and arranging for Nóra and the girls to move back into their previous apartment on Poszonyi út, a gaze across the crowded, and rather inebriated, room of a book publication party for a former colleague revealed the figure of a rather lovely, twenty-six-year-old television producer by the name of Enikö Rupp, with whom Vajda had worked on a documentary years before.

"Well, what are *you* doing here?" he breezed across the room to ask.

"What else?" the rather vivacious, and decidedly unsubtle, young woman replied. "I'm looking for you." The news of the Vajdas' marital collapse, and of András's miraculous recovery, had already reached Enikö's ears, and she had come to the party with the very hope of facilitating the encounter of which she now was an enthusiastic part. Several glasses of white wine later, the two of them were on their way out to door toward Vajda's newly-rented flat to try out Vajda's resurrected testes, and a certain renewed, and reconstellated, equilibrium in the Vajda marriage was once again on its way to being achieved.

All is well in the world, Vajda thought to himself as he and his girlfriend-to-be walked along the Danube in the direction of his flat. Yes, all was well, and—in a world where love was change, and change was the fuel that lubricated love's often-creaky wheels—all would remain well, at least for a while.

For Bergmann, meanwhile, all this news of marital disintegrations and realignments had found a rather ambivalent target by the time it reached his ears. From the window of the study of his small summer house in Hegymagas, he watched as his wife folded a mixture of one third horse manure, one third compost and one third Hungarian soil into the unpromisingly sand-and-clay-like surface of what she hoped would become her herb garden.

He still longed for passion, for the chance to light, somewhere, the embers that continued to burn within him, and, as he watched his wife's thin body stoop to mix yet anther shovelful of her mixture into the dry Hungarian earth, the face of Vajda's daughter Zsuzsa, and of all the desires she embodied, once again rose before him, and he, too, longed to be resurrected—to be borne aloft once more on the wings of desires which brought so much misery, and so much hope, to this imperfect world.

THE LIFE YOU HATE MAY BE YOUR OWN

It was almost as soon as the young girl and her mother boarded the bus heading from Budapest to Vienna that the young man reading in the seat behind them realized that he hated the child. There was something about her whiney voice, the supplicating and almost desperate tone in which she addressed her mother, that aroused something almost primal in him, and now, as he shifted uncomfortably in his seat on the double decker's upper level, he felt an accelerating rage, indeed a repugnance for the curly-haired not-yet-adolescent who sat in front of him.

"Ach, Mutti, ich bin so froh dass Du endlich gekommen bist . . . Ich habe mir solche Sorgen gemacht," "Oh, mom, I'm so happy that you are finally here . . . I was soooo worried," the child whined, her lips arcing down toward her chin as if she were about to burst into tears. Added to the almost intolerably high-pitched squeal of her voice was the fact that—unlike most pre-pubescent girls, who seemed to the young man like vast fields of tulips about to burst into flower—the girl had a prematurely middle-aged look about her, a kind of sexlessness and domesticity to her demeanor

that foreshadowed a shrewish 40-year-old, rather than a gorgeous, buttery-skinned teenager on the edge of her sexual maturity.

As the bus headed across the Danube and up into the green hills of Buda, the girl began relentlessly caressing her mother's hair, occasionally planting kisses on the older woman's forehead. The mother, too, seemed prematurely old for a woman with such a young child (perhaps, it occurred to the young man, she was actually the girl's *grand*mother?), and it was perhaps, he now thought to himself, his own history as the adopted child of much older parents that now aroused in him such an untoward animosity for the seemingly innocent girl seated before him.

"Mutti, dauert es lange bis wir in Wien ankommen?" whined the impatient child, turning her face halfway toward him as she stroked the older woman's left arm. The man and woman seated across the aisle from the pair—who, he had gathered from an earlier conversation, must be the child's aunt and uncle— wriggled uncomfortably in their seats, as if in embarrassment at their niece's irritating demeanor. The man, whose small, seagull-shaped moustache and bald head gave the impression of a more-than-usual stiffness and lack of spontaneity, seemed particularly irked by the girl's relentless whining and plaintive tone, and was making what seemed almost a too intense effort to look straight ahead into the flower-bedecked hat of the woman in front of him. Quite obviously, they had both been through numerous similar trips with the girl in the past, and knew, by now, more or less what to expect.

For the young man seated behind her, however, no such previous rehearsals muted the intensity of the disgust he now felt. And, as the bus sped along Hungarian highway M-1 toward Tatabanya and Györ, he felt a mounting desire to inflict some terrible hurt upon the small, curly-haired bundle that sat before him in order, finally, to silence her. The thoughts that passed through his mind filled him, as he reflected on them, with both repugnance and delight—repugnance in that his self-image as a kind, artistic, gentle sort of man was called into question; delight in that the thought, for example, of tying the child to the seat in front of him and then stifling her imploratory cries forever with a pillow filled him, somehow, with the precise sense of relief one feels on having a terrible nuisance finally removed from one's life.

"Mutti, ich habe so sehr hunger," "Momma, I am soooo hungry," whined the girl, stroking her mother's hair again and turning to face the young man who was, at that very moment, gleefully fantasizing about her demise. Clearly, she hoped to find from him as well some source of affirmation or, at least, friendliness. But none was forthcoming. He merely aimed a severe and uncommunicative stare in her direction, which only made her stroke and caress her mother with renewed intensity.

What enraged him so about this seemingly harmless creature? he wondered. What made her very voice fill him with such anger that his clenched fists shook at its very sound? He didn't exactly know. And yet, somehow, the image of himself as a six-year-old kindergarten student clinging so tenaciously to his mother that the principal had to be summoned daily to separate them flitted across his mind, as did, then, his mother's death when he was only ten. And he realized—though without really internalizing the insight—that there was, perhaps, some connection between his inordinate dislike for this child and the shame he had felt at his own childhood neediness and bereavement.

But, at the moment, the intensity of that emotion—roused though it may have been by some primal and narcissistic wound of his own—was so great that it largely defied such objective and self-conscious analysis, as he attempted to settle back into his seat and continue reading Tolstoy's *The Kreutzer Sonata,* he found he could concentrate on nothing else but his animosity toward this young girl. Like an insect crawling across a television screen or the sound of a ticking clock to an insomniac, she so blighted his concentration, so interfered with his peace of mind, that he could think only of somehow annihilating her from his consciousness. The four-hour-long bus trip would simply be intolerable if he had to continue listening to her supplications, had to continue staring at her grim, asexual visage before him.

When the bus stopped outside Bratislava at the Austrian border for passport and baggage inspection, the young man—by now filled with such restlessness and loathing he could hardly contain himself—literally raced from the bus and into the border station, hoping that a few moments' reprieve from the girl's proximity might at least sufficiently calm him to allow him to endure the remainder of the trip. Once inside, he carefully averted his eyes from the door or other public areas, and merely sat on a stool at the snack bar sipping coffee and gazing at the blank wall. When the call came to board the bus once more, he raced, face down, for the door and into his seat, hoping for a few further moments of peace before the girl and her mother returned. He would, of course, gladly have changed seats, so as to remove himself physically from the distasteful creature, but the bus was entirely sold out, being one-hundred forints cheaper than the train and significantly more reliable.

The girl and her mother, closely followed by her chagrined-looking aunt and uncle, were virtually the last to re-enter the bus, and—as she brushed past the young man's self-consciously averted gaze—he could not help but notice her short, bright red skirt and thinking what a strange juxtaposition it presented to her pronouncedly sexless, middle-aged features, observing once again that the girl seemed to him not merely psychologically repugnant, but a kind of circus freak, a caricature of the attractiveness and incipient sexuality he usually associated with girls her age.

It already seemed like days, rather than hours, since the bus had pulled out of Budapest's East Terminal, and as he attempted to settle back into his seat for the last hour of the journey, he resolved to dwell a bit on precisely what it was that made the young girl so hateful to him, to see if he couldn't arouse—out of what he felt to be his genuinely empathic nature—a scintilla of human sympathy for her. Though himself a scholar and a rising young professor of 19th century literature—in particular, the novels of Tolstoy and Dostoyevsky—he had occasionally flirted with the idea of entering one of the so-called "helping" professions—psychology or even social work—and it was partly for this reason that his present lack of sympathy, indeed his unmitigated disdain, for the obviously needy child troubled him, colliding with his own self-image. Yet there was, at the same time, something invigorating, almost joyful, about this feeling, a passionate intensity and sense of possession not unlike the one he had felt in moments of love and rapture. So he felt, at the same time, delighted and disturbed, affirmed and called into question, disappointed and intoxicated, repulsed and aroused.

"Mutti, können wir in Wien etwas zu essen kaufen—bitte, bitte? "Momma, can we buy something to eat when we get to Vienna—please, oh please?" implored the child. It was, perhaps, also the sound of these implorations in the language of his own childhood that so reverberated with some deep inner anger, he thought. It might, he speculated, be the sight and sound of this child—needy, vulnerable, German-speaking, with seemingly only one parent (in other words, much as he once was)—that aroused

such violent emotions now. He *must,* he told himself, get a grip on his anger, attempt to understand it, recognize the fact that this inordinate rage was not exclusively of the child's making.

The uncle had by now, his niece's incessant chattering notwithstanding, fallen asleep, and the child, seeming much annoyed at having the audience for her whinings diminished by one, accelerated the pace of her questions and complaints as if to compensate.

"Ach, Mutti, ich bin soooo sehr müde—Kommen wir nicht bald an?" "Oh, momma, I am soooo very tired—Will we be there soon?" She now planted a long flurry of kisses on the older woman's forehead, rising up on her knees on the seat to do so, while again trying to catch the young man's eye. Having by now ruminated on the sources of his rage, he tried as best he could to force a half-smile in the girl's direction, a gesture that—at least judging from her pained look and the increasing frenzy of her overtures toward her mother—proved an abysmal failure.

He began, now, to think of the neediness of his own childhood, of how often, after his mother's death he had longed to whine that same irritating whine, make those same desperate entreaties for affection that now, in the shape of the young girl kneeling on the seat in front of him, so strongly aroused his hatred and rage. He remembered, just as the bus pulled onto the Ringstrasse near the blazing lights of the Opera House, those numerous Saturday afternoons of his childhood when he had stood with his father in the *Stehgallerie* of the Metropolitan Opera House, a ten-year-old motherless boy longing for a woman's affections, longing to be cured of a grief he could not yet name.

So deeply was he entranced in these thoughts that he hardly noticed that the bus had pulled away from the Ring and down Weiskirchnerstrasse, coming to a halt in the bus terminal parking lot. He had not noticed, even, that the girl and her family had already disembarked from the bus, so that when the driver tapped him on the shoulder with the words, *"Bitte alle aussteigen—Wir sind in Wien!"* he was seated completely alone on the bus's upper tier, all the other passengers having already disappeared down the steps and into the parking lot.

He gathered his belongings from the overhead compartment and hurried down the stairs, wishing he had been able to force even a halfhearted smile or a single kind word in the child's direction. Outside, it was a cool August night, the lights of the Ringstrasse glistening from around the corner and a faint, sweet smell that seemed to him almost like *Schlagsahne* in the air. Gazing rather vacantly now toward the parking lot's perimeter, he could just faintly distinguish the outline of a short red skirt, ruffling in the wind like a matador's cape, as—her crippled right leg splayed awkwardly outwards away from her mother—the young girl half turned, almost as if to face him, and disappeared beneath the bright Viennese moon.

Michael Blumenthal

HE HAD TRIED

He had tried with whores from so many different countries and venues—French whores, Hungarian whores, German whores, Israeli (that is to say, mostly Russian) ones. He had tried with whores from the escort services and whores from the "night clubs," whores from the downtown streets of Budapest and Berlin, and whores from little Eastern European country roads wearing green Day-Glo halter tops and Sony Walkmen and chugging large bottles of bottled water in the blown Saran Wrap of summer heat waves.

He had tried on his back and on all fours, he had tried from up above and from underneath, he had tried with the help of lubricants and surgical gloves, he had tried with his nose up various orifices and with his organ stroked by his own, and other, hands, so seemingly warm and capable. He had tried in leotards and G-strings, in panty hose and expensive lingerie. He had tried while praying and while cursing, while talking dirty and while speaking in tongues. He had tried while moaning, and while remaining silent, he had tried with the help of chemicals and abetted by supplements and organic vegetables. He had tried in the wee hours of early morning, and in the to-him-uneroticized hours of late night. He had tried, even, in the afternoons, as well in the dusk-encumbered hours *("cinq à sept")* recommended by French novelists and sexologists.

He had tried and he had tried, and he was trying now, lying on his back with his legs thrown over his head while a young French blond named Patricia whose ad for *"lutte mixte vraiment érotique"* he had answered the previous day massaged his prostrate gland with two, lubricant-supplemented fingers and impatiently interrogated him—*"Tu viens? Ça te plait? Tu veux quelque chose d'autre?"* Then, at his insistence, she mounted him, as they called it back home, in the "rimming" position and allowed him to richly inhale, without the wished-for dénouement, the imaginary odors of her freshly-washed rectum and vagina. And he had tried again.

"Est-ce que vous avez un problème avec la jouissance, monsieur?" Patricia demanded, rapidly losing some of the pre-programmed charm and warmth she had exhibited when he first entered the door and handed her the two-hundred euros she had discretely but firmly asked for *"avant qu'on commence."*

Yes, he had tried hard—was, in fact, this very minute trying hard, and been trying hard now for some fifteen years—but the only thing he had to show for all his huffing and puffing and cross-dressing and lubricating and mirror-scanning and inhaling was a rapidly emptying bank account (in several countries) and a somewhat pleasant tingling in his rectum—the place where, according to Yeats, "love has pitched its tent"—and which even the greatest of pleasure-seekers (whom, sadly, he was not among) would hardly have considered worth the accumulated investment.

He had tried with two wives—with the first of whom he

had wonderful sex, but no love, the second with whom he had considerable *tendresse*, but hardly any sex. He had tried *en plein air* and in waterbeds and he had tried on orthopedic mattresses and futons of various kinds and textures. He had tried with scented massage oils and with flavored lubricants, he had tried, even, with chocolate pudding (which he loved) and the lovely Hungarian cottage cheese known as *túro*.

He had tried with stewardesses and waitresses and with high school girls and babysitters. He had tried with lap dancers and gymnasts and ski bunnies and orthodontists. He had tried, even, with his high school biology teacher, Mrs. Green, when she looked up at him while dissecting a frog and he blew a kiss at her through a haze of Bunsen burners and fondled her kneecaps.

He had tried with certain friends' wives, and he had tried with their sisters and cousins and concubines and surgical assistants. He had tried with his wife's sister and with his own second cousin, he had tried with the lifeguard and the night watchwoman and the insurance adjuster and rental agent. He had tried with the speechless and with the overzealous, and he had tried with the Children of Israel and with the Children of Palestine. He had tried near the Wailing Wall and he had tried beside a bower bird's nest in the wilds of Australia. He had tried in the Galapagos, beside the blue boobies and iguanas and Galapagos penguins. He had tried in Huehuetenango and Antigua and Chichicastenango and Tikal and Guatemala City. He had tried at Lake Atitlan and Lake Balaton and Lake Como and Lake Ontario. He had tried, even, at Lake Winnepesaukee, uninspired venue though it was.

Once, he had even tried in the bathroom of a Boeing 737, with a girl from Weston, Connecticut whose name—wasn't it Kristin something?—he had long forgotten. "Is something wrong?" said the stewardess, when they emerged looking rather seasick. But nothing was wrong: He had tried. He had really tried.

He had tried for charity's sake and for goodness's and for vanity's and for boredom's. He had tried with a philanthropist's generosity, and with the restraint of a miser. He had tried by pumping a fist into the air like an Olympic athlete, and had tried by massaging his star of David, and then the rabbit's foot in his pocket. He had tried by citing the Old Testament, and then by reading the New One, he had tried with the Baghavad Gita and the Koran and the Tibetan Book of the Dead and the Talmud.

He had tried in bad weather, and he had tried—even harder—in sunshine. He had tried on the crystal-clear sands of Bermuda and the white beaches of Bali. He had tried while inhaling the tropical odors of St. John in the Caribbean, and under the influence of fresh *ganja* weed on the shores of Cinnamon Bay in Jamaica.

"You're trying too hard," a Ukrainian whore in her bright red string underwear advised him in Bucharest. "Just relax, it will happen." So he had tried—hard—relaxing, but nothing had come of it.

He had tried the Alexander Technique, and he had tried— oh so painfully!—with Rolfing. He had tried homoeopathic medications and transcendental meditation. He had tried with the Tantric guidebooks, and he had tried, even, at the Naropa Institute, along with the Disembodied Poets. He had tried at Esalen and Kripalu, and at the *clubs échangeistes* of Paris and Cap d'Aigues. He had tried with threesomes and foursomes and had tried, most frequently, amid the loneliness of twosomes.

He had even tried, last summer, with two of the eight Swedish widows studying yoga at the house next door . . . tried very hard, broken English and all. "To Martin," one had left him a note along with her recently deceased father's hat that he had so unsubtly coveted. "Take care of your head, and wear this hat in the sun. Nice to have meeting you. Good luck and so long."

Good luck and so long. It might as well have been the refrain to the sputtering symphony of his life. *Good luck and so long.*

But he didn't want that as his refrain, his swan song, his little lullaby of failure and longing. What a crock of shit! *Good luck and so long.* What ever had happened to *Hi there! It's great to have you*? What ever had happened to *This is it, baby! This is it!*? What ever had happened to the successful, though ramshackle, music of two bodies singing together the same lovely, stuttering songs of flesh and disequilibrium?

"I simply had the feeling that this relationship, for both of us, was no longer what it had been," his Hungarian girlfriend had recently written to him, "and I had also quite simply had enough of hearing your ceaseless remarks and innuendos about my not loving you enough, not supporting you enough, etc. etc. The final straw for me was that horribly unpleasant evening with your friends at the *Bagloyvar*, where you kept scolding and trying to provoke me."

And oh, dear God, how he had tried with her.

He had perhaps, it occurred to him now, not tried hard enough—he who had wanted, in his life, so badly, both sex *and* love, passion and the solace of the heart. And now *this* was what he ultimately had, this stranger rubbing up and down on his heavily lubricated prick like a ceramicist wetting down her clay or a domestic servant removing grease from a corroded household pipe.

It was this he now had, this stranger who had wrestled him to the ground for 200 Euros an hour, and who was now sitting on his face so that it was only with difficulty that he could breathe at all. *It was this*, he mused to himself sadly, *it was only this*, and now, for the love of God, it was his.

THE LETTER

She had met him, as she now remembered it, at her apartment—or was it someone else's?—in Ithaca, New York back in the early 1970s. He was teaching French at a local high school, and she was impressed because she had been to France twice as an exchange student, once in high school and once in college. She wasn't French by birth, but thought the language was neat, and thought she had finally met someone with whom she had something unique in common. Plus most of the other college seniors she knew, unlike him, seemed lacking in depth.

It seemed funny, now, to think how, whenever she started sharing stories of her sex life with close girlfriends, she would always say, "I once had sex with a guy in Ithaca who was very, very, very, very, very, very smart." That's all she'd say, because that's all she knew . . . or, at least, all she remembered.

He had seemed eager to have her come over, but in a very serious way, not light-hearted. He had an apartment all to himself, which had also impressed her because most students she knew had crash pads that housed too many bodies. He also had a cat, who had lain down between her breasts. He himself had been very determined to do the deed, and was quite bossy about it, while she was very passive, shy and inexperienced. What had really humiliated her at the time was that she wore panties that were cotton and came up to her waist (she wasn't a virgin but so naïve!) and he had reprimanded her, saying guys were turned off by that, that she should have worn silky bikini panties. He seemed mad and annoyed, but carried on with what he wanted to do to her despite. She didn't hold it against him now; it was just that the memory was so strong, how guilty and inadequate she had felt at the time. She could laugh at it now!

Seeming distant, businesslike and cold, he had left for work early in the morning, telling her to simply close the door behind her when she left. It was only then, after he was gone, that she had truly begun to enjoy herself. She had already realized the previous evening that he was out of her league—he was so bright, and clearly on his way to bigger and better things—but now, for the first time in years, she had an entire household to herself, along with the beautiful fattish cat, named Emily (after Emily Dickinson, he had told her), who, unlike him, seemed quite enamored of her and lay down between her breasts on the bed after he was gone.

After she got up and treated herself to a shower, she suddenly (perhaps something inside her already knew) felt very domestic and decided to clean the kitchen—it clearly could use a woman's touch. Scrubbing the oven and refrigerator, she found herself whistling and humming and trying to find things to prolong her stay, since she knew she would never be back. She even began, despite herself, to fantasize about being married and living in a big house with a big kitchen. Maybe it had been the female hormones already kicking in.

Before leaving, she had gone through his medicine chest, checked out his large supply of condoms—apparently never used—and the various lubricants for all sorts of orifices and positions he kept in the drawer. Then—perhaps out of anger, perhaps it was merely longing, she really couldn't recall—she had buried her long cotton panties in his underwear drawer and, reluctantly, let herself out.

Later, she had initially ignored the clues when her period didn't come. She had been dancing in a production, and preferred not to think about it. Finally, her roommate told her to face reality. She gave her the $150 for the abortion and drove her down to NYC to the one legal clinic that existed back then and practically made her get rid of it. She hadn't stepped back at the time to think through the situation. It simply didn't compute. She knew she had to graduate, that was it.

But the most poignant thing about it—and a poem could be written about this, she now thought—was that her sister had gotten pregnant at the exact same time. She went on to have a wonderful son, who became so connected to her spiritually that they always felt *they* should have been mother and son, or at least brother and sister. Her sister had always said that she and Jack would have been like two peas in a pod and fantastic exploring partners (they both liked to hunt in swamps for turtles and such) if they had been siblings. Today, Jack was still a nature child, a child of 60s hippies, and his life had somehow developed in parallel with her own.

She had moved to Oregon in 1974 and done the hippie commune thing, while her sister stayed on the East Coast and lived a very conventional life. Jack always said he wished he could have been *her* son and lived in communes while growing up. He was into radical environmentalism now, and was busily writing a book.

Both she and Jack believed very strongly in life after death and that we choose the parents we want to be born through. They had both come to believe that Jack wanted to be born through her, and was calling from his spirit-world self for her to get pregnant.

But when she decided to get the abortion, his spirit, she felt, had left her fetus and gone over to her closest relative in order to come to life and be as close as possible to her, since the first route hadn't worked out.

If only she had thought of her own pregnancy as something that special! That a soul mate wanted to come to her, to ease her loneliness, to fill her life with joy and happiness! If only she had seen the possibilities, the preciousness of that deeply convoluted life and of her own, before going to have that abortion! As it was, Jack had a very lonely childhood, and she herself had a barren marriage and didn't see him for another twenty-five years.

Her later life had been very unhappy, because her idealism and naiveté caused her to devote twenty years to a strict religious cult, where she had been given a mate she didn't even like but whom she believed God wanted her to have to make her suffer her atonement. Her husband was infertile, so they didn't have children, which remained a huge source of grief for her, particularly because the church she had joined decreed that salvation was measured by how many children you raised to Christ. She could only think she must have displeased God greatly.

It was very interesting to her that Jack went on to have a parallel life to her own. They had both been raised in Chicago, but went to California when they became engulfed and brainwashed by a fundamentalist cult and given a spouse—no love, no children— and were both indoctrinated near to each other (he in Berkeley, she in Monterey) about twenty years apart. Now, they were both out of their respective cults and both living in Ann Arbor. Her sister was living there too. She had gone back to school later and graduated cum laude in Philosophy (M.A.) and Jack was writing his book on . . . well, something about how off-track our civilization was, or at least that was how he described it.

She hadn't really thought of him, or of that long-ago night in Ithaca, for a long, long time, and it was only last year when she got on the internet and someone (her sister) said why not look up people you have known, to see where they are at. So she had typed in Martin Weinstock and what a surprise! She read his poem, positioned just after the forward in a book called *The Story of Your Life*. She hadn't started the book yet, but she knew that she, too, needed to "rise from the bleak island of my old story and tread my way home." And now she felt like writing to him because he was a poet, no doubt with deep sensibilities, so she knew he would find her story interesting.

She knew, according to his book, that he had had several potential offspring that were aborted—a fact that, now, both angered and depressed her—and that he hadn't been ready to be a father because his own relationship with his parents had been so tangled. Her own abortion, no doubt, would have hardly mattered to him anyway . . . it would merely have been just one more. He probably would never even have known he had a son if she had brought their child to term. She had never seen him again after that one night, nor had she wanted to look him up either, because she was rather intimidated and scared of him. Did he recall, now, who she was or what happened? No, she had probably simply melded in with an endless string of other one-night stands and aborted pregnancies. She had probably been for him nothing more than another notch in his belt.

In many ways she wished she could write the story of her life, as he had his, but she couldn't use the computer much anymore. But now she felt like looking back, even though she was not so mentally alert anymore (there was Alzheimer's in her family and it was creeping up on her, too). Before she lost her memory entirely, she wanted to write to him so he would know this little part of his own history, however insignificant—or entirely forgotten—it may have been to him, and it would become part of *his* memory and carry on for a few more years at least.

She understood that he now lived in Paris. She had visited Paris once and really enjoyed it. She hoped he was doing well. She didn't expect him to write back or anything, but she hoped he would get her letter, and that it might slip into his mind and make him realize, too, how significant his life was, and the many streams it flowed into.

Now she wanted to read *The Story of Your Life* and attempt to re-story herself, so as not to feel bogged down by regrets. *What if? What if?* Such thoughts could be a killer. Her life hadn't at all turned out the way she had wanted it to but she hoped she could come to terms with it. She was glad she still had enough memory left to share this with him (Jack and she hadn't even told his mother the story). She hoped he was enjoying being a father to his son. She hoped that—sometime, somewhere—he had found her cotton underwear in that drawer, mingled happily with his own.

BOOKS FROM ETRUSCAN

Zarathustra Must Die | Dorian Alexander

The Disappearance of Seth | Kazim Ali

Drift Ice | Jennifer Atkinson

Crow Man | Tom Bailey

Coronology | Claire Bateman

What We Ask of Flesh | Remica L. Bingham

No Hurry | Michael Blumenthal

Choir of the Wells | Bruce Bond

Cinder | Bruce Bond

Peal | Bruce Bond

Toucans in the Arctic | Scott Coffel

Body of a Dancer | Renée E. D'Aoust

Scything Grace | Sean Thomas Dougherty

Nahoonkara | Peter Grandbois

The Confessions of Doc Williams & Other Poems | William Heyen

The Football Corporations | William Heyen

A Poetics of Hiroshima | William Heyen

Shoah Train | William Heyen

September 11, 2001, American Writers Respond | Edited by William Heyen

As Easy As Lying | H. L. Hix

As Much As, If Not More Than | H. L. Hix

Chromatic | H. L. Hix

First Fire, Then Birds | H. L. Hix

God Bless | H. L. Hix

Incident Light | H. L. Hix

Legible Heavens | H. L. Hix

Lines of Inquiry | H. L. Hix

Shadows of Houses | H. L. Hix

Etruscan Press Is Proud of Support Received From

Wilkes University

Youngstown State University

The Raymond John Wean Foundation

The Ohio Arts Council

The Stephen & Jeryl Oristaglio Foundation

The Nathalie & James Andrews Foundation

The National Endowment for the Arts

The Ruth H. Beecher Foundation

The Bates-Manzano Fund

The New Mexico Community Foundation

Drs. Barbara Brothers & Gratia Murphy Fund

Founded in 2001 with a generous grant from the Oristaglio Foundation, Etruscan Press is a nonprofit cooperative of poets and writers working to produce and promote books that nurture the dialogue among genres, achieve a distinctive voice, and reshape the literary and cultural histories of which we are a part.

etruscan press
www.etruscanpress.org

Etruscan Press books may be ordered from

Consortium Book Sales and Distribution
800.283.3572
www.cbsd.com

Small Press Distribution
800.869.7553
www.spdbooks.org